Stealing the Troll's Heart

Trollkin Lovers

Book One

Lyonne Riley

CHAPTER 1

TELISE

I n my world, if you don't eat first, you become the meal. You must have the fastest feet in the woods, the quickest slash with a knife, and the sharpest mind to survive.

Luckily, that's me. I live in shadows. I learned early how to walk silently, to disguise myself like part of the scenery. I kill before I'm killed. That's how I've lived this long, anyway.

I don't come out to the Sandteeth often, but there's just some things you can't get back home. Most importantly—the Wicke's Leopard. It's a tricky bastard to find, for the same reason that its hide is so valuable: Its fur is made to blend into any background perfectly, rendering the wearer of it invisible. If I could get lucky and lay my hands on one, maybe two specimens, the sale of a single cloak could clothe and feed me for a few years, and my trip will be completely worthwhile.

It wasn't a cheap or a quick trip, either: I took a caravan and did a two-week stint on a ship just to get to this forsaken place. The mountains are tall and pointed like fangs, and the landscape is unforgiving. I'm glad I brought my own supplies, or enough of them to last me a week before I'll have to turn around and restock in town.

I've had my eye on some droppings for a while. I found them last night and was certain they belonged to my leopard. There are wolves here too, but my hunter's sense says the shape and stink is right for a big cat.

And yet I've been standing in this one spot, watching, for most of the day now without any sign of my prey. Perhaps it was just passing through and doesn't plan to return this way again. Damn.

No, no, it's too soon to give up. I have to wait until after sunset, because that's when the leopards will become most active again.

Rustle.

The shaking of some leaves nearby gives me a start. I make sure the foliage is covering me, especially any metal parts that might reflect the light, and peer out.

Crunch.

It's a heavy footstep, certainly no leopard. From my vantage point all I can see are a pair of legs and big, thick boots. Another crunch as the heel sends a pebble flying toward me.

"*Groken,*" a voice says. It's low and guttural. I know who it belongs to right away. "*Savegg kog.*"

Trollkin. I'd be able to pick out their barbaric language anywhere. It reminds me of mushy potatoes, all squished and slurred together until the words themselves are nearly indiscernible.

Someone else approaches from behind. One of his trollkin buddies. Supposedly there are differences among them, but to me, they're all the same: Enemies.

I've slit more than one trollkin throat, just like I've slit other human throats. My parents would certainly disapprove if they knew how often I found myself in a tete-a-tete with someone who wants to murder me. But that's how you make it big. You have to be willing to take risks, and I'm nothing if not a thrill-seeker.

The trollkin stomp onward, and now that they've disturbed this area, there's no way my leopard is coming back anytime soon. So I retreat into the bushes and head for a nearby tree. I want to get an idea of who they are and what they're carrying. Sometimes the easiest way to a good meal is by stealing it off of someone else.

One is blue and one is green, I can tell that much from here. And they're both carrying money and supplies. The green one is shorter, with little tusks that pull his lips back. The bluish one is taller, with wild, dark red hair and some of it braided, the rest falling into his eyes as he walks. His tusks are longer, more curled. He has a looseness to him, like he doesn't have a care in the world.

That beast will change his tune pretty soon.

I jog on ahead of them, aiming for a tree that they'll have to walk right underneath. I'm not sure why they're out here trekking through the woods, when the nearest road is a good five miles off—and then I wonder if perhaps they're here for the same reason that I am.

The last thing I need is competition. I'd better end this if I can.

Once I reach the tree, I clamber up as quickly and quietly as possible. Barely a leaf shivers under me. I gingerly walk out onto a branch, testing my balance as I go. When I'm as far as I think the branch can bear, I stop moving and reach down to steady myself.

In just a few moments, the two trollkin approach my position. One carries a blunderbuss, the other a rather large axe. The battle axe is both incredibly deadly and mighty unwieldy, so he'll have a hard time hitting me with it given how fast I can move. The blunderbuss might prove a more significant issue, but it's still big enough that he'll need time to ready it, and I'll have my window to escape.

I should take out the green one before the blue one can even pull out his weapon, but something tells me the blue one is more dangerous. It's the way he walks with a swagger, and holds himself like he's relaxing on the beach, but every bare inch of his body is hard muscle and tense sinew. He has large tusks that emerge from each side of his mouth at an angle, with deadly points that curl up in front of him. He could gut a pig with one of those. That's when I notice he's swinging a little hatchet around in his hand as if to entertain himself, and I wouldn't want to be on the receiving end of it. It might only be the size of his hand, but it would easily cleave me through the chest and bring an end to my long series of wins.

Then, they're underneath me. Finally. I drop from the branch like one of my leopard prey, right onto the blue one's head. I aim with one foot, and he gets a real bonk to the noggin. He stumbles backwards, clutching his face.

"*Kaggen!*" He's irate as I drop to the ground. The green one is already pulling out his blunderbuss, but he's not fast enough. I swing one leg as hard as I can into the back of his knee. I wouldn't be strong enough on my own to take him down, but if you can aim for a weak spot...

The green one falls to the ground, also cursing. I leap at the blue one again as he struggles to regain his balance and bring the point of my knife to his throat.

Click.

Before I can bury the dagger into the troll's flesh, I find the big mouth of the blunderbuss right up against the side of my head.

Raz'jin

"Blizzek, are we any closer?" I'm growing impatient with all this tromping through the woods.

We make an unlikely pair of trollkin, Blizzek and I, but our partnership works well enough. He comes equipped with a handy ore detector, which he's holding up now to measure if we're still going the right way. The indicator wiggles around at the halfway point. When he turns it one direction, the indicator flies upward.

"That way," he says, pointing.

There had been talk of gold in this area, but it was just talk. I wanted to see it for myself and evaluate if we could strike it rich, so we took some horses and crossed the wide-open plains for these abysmal mountains.

We've been wandering around the woods for days now, and finally this morning we got a read. Now we just have to find where it's buried and hope it's not too far down to get to. If we find something but can't extract it, we might be able to sell off the mining rights for a pretty penny.

First come, first find and all.

There aren't a lot of creatures out in the Sandteeth besides birds, rabbits, and a few big cats, but I could swear that I see something move out of the corner of my eye. A flash of something metallic, a small face. But before I can turn my head, it's gone.

Must have been a deer.

But a few paces later, I realize it was no deer. There's a ball of something dark falling from above, and I receive a massive blow to the head that sends me stumbling backwards. Pain shoots through my skull. When I regain my balance, there's a tiny, metal point pressed against my throat.

I stop moving instantly. There's a human woman standing in front of me, her dagger ready to plunge through my neck. I've taken a lot of hits—my scars are my proof—but I wouldn't survive that one.

Blizzek is on one knee, blunderbuss held out with the horn pressed against the side of the human's head.

Stalemate.

The human is panting, her bright green eyes glowing like whole emeralds. Not much of her skin is visible under her jerkin and long leather pants, but what I can see is pale and freckled. She hollers something in her language at us, first at me, and then at Blizzek.

"Can't understand a word," I say to him, pretending there's not a dagger pointed at my throat. I can't let her think she's got me scared.

"Probably bargaining for her life," he says. He presses the blunderbuss more firmly against the woman's head, and she falls still. Some of her red hair slips out of the tie at the top of her head, tumbling in front of her eyes. The fierce look on her face shows me that she's a killer; that she's taken before and will take again if we give her the chance.

Damn. She's kind of hot.

"It'd be my life, too," I say. "You shoot that gun and I'm gutted like a fish."

Blizzek cocks the gun, but the girl doesn't flinch.

"That was a bad call on your part, Raz," he says. "Letting a little thing get one over on you like that."

My only option might be to work something out with her. Convince her we're going to let her go, and then go in

6

for the kill when she thinks she's free. I might not even end her life right away. Someone back in Hargoth might want to buy her. It would be up to them what to do with her after that.

Such a pretty creature, though. It would be a shame to see her covered in mud with a chain around her ankle or tied to some orc's bed.

I slowly raise my hands in surrender. The tip of the dagger presses even further in, barely nicking my skin. She's quite serious, I can tell that much.

"Can we figure this out?" I ask her. "A truce, maybe?"

She just narrows her eyes at me, clearly not understanding what I'm asking. I'm sure she only speaks Freysian, the language the humans have always used.

I gesture to the ground. The human never takes her eyes off of me.

"Put down weapons," I say slower, as if that will help her understand. "Go our separate ways."

I reach for my hand axe, and she digs deeper with her knife. I choke a little.

"It's all right." I try to use a soothing voice. When I slide the axe out of its holster, I drop it to the ground. Then I hold out a hand. "Let's put the weapons down. Okay?"

She would be an idiot to fall for this, but I can see she's considering it. She doesn't have a way out of this, either. The only one who might survive would be Blizzek. This would be a really stupid way to go out—a tiny pretty thing getting a dagger through my esophagus.

Then she says something I can't distinguish, and releases some of the tension between the dagger and my flesh.

"I think she's going to back off," I say to Blizzek. "Make it seem like you're going to put your gun down."

He frowns at me. "What? No way."

"If you don't, one of us is going to die, and I will haunt you for the rest of your life if I'm the one who goes down."

Suddenly the human shouts something at me. She doesn't like us talking past her. She gestures with the dagger, and I swallow hard, hoping she doesn't make a mistake that close to my jugular.

Blizzek gives me one last withering look before he starts to remove the horn of his gun from the girl's head.

She's quicker than lightning. The moment the gun isn't on top of her, she's already moving, and she kicks Blizzek square in the balls. He shouts and drops his gun, like a giant idiot.

I reach out and grab whatever I can—and my hand wraps around her tiny arm. The girl looks up at me, green eyes wild, and snarls something in her language. I reach for the axe over my back. Her time on this plane is over. That's when she grabs one of my tusks in her other hand and yanks my head towards hers.

For a split second, I'm looking deep into her green eyes, right before she presses her lips to mine. They're pliable and small, and I find my hand freezing on the handle of my axe.

In that one lost second, she pulls away from me, her skinny wrist slipping out of my hand. And then she's running. Before either of us can recover, she dives into the woods at twice the speed we could chase her and vanishes like a shadow.

"Raz'jin!" Blizzek waves his arms at me. Then he clutches his crotch in agony. "What the hell?"

"I don't know. Ask her!" I'm enraged. Right in front of Blizzek, a human woman *kissed me*? And then she used my surprise to escape.

"You let her get away." He scowls deeply. "She pulled a stupid, easy trick and you let her get away with it."

"I'm sorry that I didn't expect *that*."

Blizzek rolls his eyes, and when he's finally recovered, we

keep on in the direction of our gold. He kicks a rock. "Would have made a nice trophy," he says.

But I'm rattled. She was so soft, but so warm, too. I found that more than anything, I wanted to bury my hands in her, and smash her body against mine.

What a dirty, nasty trick from a dirty, nasty creature.

CHAPTER 2

TELISE

Hours later, I'm still not sure why I did it.

I keep telling myself that it worked. I got away, right? I'd done something unexpected, and it took the troll by surprise enough that I was able to make my escape. Otherwise, he would have cut me in half with that axe.

But the more I try to rationalize it away, the more that I'm thinking about what his mouth felt like. It was only a split second, but I found something in that second that I didn't expect to find.

Well, maybe I should have expected it. Deleran has always called me "odd". He's my only real friend, but he's back in the king's city of Culberra doing only gods know what. Probably drinking himself under a table, with women crawling all over him, each wanting a taste of him.

"You've never made a move on me in all the years that I've

known you," he said once. We met as kids back in our hometown of Great Oak but left together to do something a little bigger. "Why not?"

"Not interested," I'd said.

"Like, in men, or in me specifically?"

"I'm just not into it." I had shrugged at the time. "Gender irrelevant."

"Who is your type, then?" Deleran asked then, but I had no answer. I felt like I'd know it when I saw it. "You're going to be a virgin forever, Telise."

But it's not that I don't have a sex drive. Oh, I do, and it's loud and angry. It's just that nothing that should turn me on ever has. No, I've been wanting something my whole life, and I just don't know what it is yet.

At least I managed to get away from the situation with the two trollkin, hide intact. Maybe it wasn't a win, but it was a tie.

I decide it better to leave this area and get a new start somewhere else, hopefully farther away from Mr. Axe and Mr. Blunderbuss. Not that I wouldn't hear them coming a mile away, but I don't want to risk another run-in after what I just did.

After setting up my next camp, it's time to scout for any signs of one of my leopards. But I'm so caught up in thinking about the strange trollkin, and the surprisingly intelligent eyes hiding under his heavy brows, that I don't notice the orcs are on me until it's too late.

RAZ'JIN

We're exhausted by the time we finish for the day. We found a pile of boulders at our destination, but after some hacking away, even blowing a charge, we couldn't find much of anything inside.

"We have to go back, bring some others with us," Blizzek says.

"It's a lost cause. We should just start over somewhere else tomorrow." What I don't want to say is that I'm afraid of running into that little human creature again. I don't like how she made me feel, not one bit. It's like a sharp pain in my side that won't stop until I pry my mind away from her.

Those feral green eyes. That pink mouth pulled back across gritted teeth. She was so angry, so ready to push that dagger through my throat. I have a bit of a hard-on just thinking about those pursed, soft lips against mine, for that split second before she made a run for it.

"Fine." My compatriot clearly isn't happy with me, and, perhaps, thinks me a coward. But I don't care. Along with our failure to find anything concrete today, I'm ready for a strong drink.

As we approach the nearby trollkin town of Hargoth, there's a loud commotion. Orcs and trolls are cheering and growling, like there's a party going on. When we step inside the wood gates, I finally see what all the fuss is about.

Her. I'd recognize that red hair anywhere now. She's strung up by her hands to a massive post, dangling a good five feet off the ground. But now her clothes are torn, so one of her two breasts is exposed to the air. She has pink nipples and the palest flesh I've ever seen. A good part of her pants are gone, too, and there are bloody cuts and bruises all over her. I can see why when someone throws a whole apple at her—but she doesn't cry out.

"It's her," says Blizzek. He howls with glee. "Well, she got what was coming to her, didn't she?"

"Sure." But I'm stuck on her, and the way her fierce face dares anyone and everyone around her to fight. Angrily she yells something at the crowd, which only fuels their fire. There are more jeers, and someone flings a beer all over her.

I can't watch this anymore. I head into the tavern, leaving Blizzek behind me.

"Raz, wait." He jogs to catch up. "What, didn't want to get one in on her? You still have a mark on your head where she kicked you."

Right. I'd almost forgotten about that. She was the one who attacked *me*.

"They should just get it over with," I say as we sit down at the bar. I shove a coin across, and the bartender hands me a beer. "Kill her, don't torture her."

Blizzek tilts his head. "Hmm." He picks up his own beer and takes a long sip. "Girlie get under your skin a little, did she?"

I roll my eyes. "No."

"That little kiss she stole, eh?" Blizzek elbows me. "That's what does it for you, is it?"

I've had my fair share of trollkin women. Orcesses, trollesses, and everything in-between. They usually gravitated to Blizzek, who's handsome as orcs come. I'm usually the friend that the less attractive women get stuck with.

And I fuck them, of course. A guy's got needs. But I'm always careful to pull out and empty myself out on top of them or in their mouths—I never put my seed anywhere it could go to use. The last thing I need is a nasty little offspring to deal with.

I don't fuck for keeps, is what I'm saying. I get my rocks off and move on, never interested in any one of them enough to stay for a second night.

"I don't have a taste for humans," I say, swishing my beer around.

Blizzek makes a disgusted face. "You're right. Maybe they should just cut her open and be done with it."

Something about the idea of an orc slicing her through at the throat fills me with a kind of horror.

I take another deep swig of my beer. Whatever they do with her is no concern of mine. She's fair game, just another piece of human scum whose head somebody can hang up above their mantelpiece.

"Another beer, please," I call out, hitting my mug on the bar.

TELISE

He was here.

For a second, the way he looked at me, I had a fleeting hope that he might come and free me. The way the troll's eyes traveled from my feet up to my breasts to my eyes, I thought he might just stride across the plaza and tear me down from the ropes holding me up.

But he didn't. He watched them pelt me with food, then turned and left.

Well, I can't really blame him. I did try to kill him.

After a while, the other orcs start to lose interest in me and wander away. Instead of facing the jeers of everyone in town, I'm left to hang from these ropes half-naked as the sun goes down. The air quickly becomes chilly, and the ropes are burning and biting into my wrists.

What a miserable way to die. Caught by fucking trollkin and strung up in the town square for ridicule. I wonder if they'll just leave me here and let me starve, or if they'll cut me down eventually and kill me by beheading. I've heard they like beheadings. If Deleran found out, he would probably make fun of me before leaving a flower on my grave.

I start to fade out of consciousness, then drift back in again, in too much pain to fall asleep properly. It feels like my hands might just come off. A little trickle of blood runs down my arm from where the rope eats into my flesh. Just great. I'll die of a blood disease out here.

Finally, I do manage to slip away into a miserable sleep. But I'm suddenly shaken awake by the sensation of my hands moving.

"*Grzzan,*" I hear a familiar voice say. Up above my head, my hands are rattling around as someone cuts through the ropes. Every time one of them moves, it burns like fire down my arms, but I hold in a cry.

It's him.

The troll has just severed one of the two ropes holding my hands in place. As my arm falls to my side, blood dribbling from my wrist, he gets to work on the other rope.

And then, suddenly both my hands are free. I fall down to the ground, my feet unable to hold themselves up.

"*Argak!*" The troll drops down from the posts and walks over. He's obviously drunk as a skunk, barely able to hold himself up. He kicks me. "*Argak!*"

Whatever that means, I get the sense he wants me to get out of there. And it's a good idea. I've been given a second chance, who knows why, and I'm not going to let it slip by.

I manage to get my legs underneath me again, and when I stand up, I find I'm looking right into his eyes—those shockingly intelligent eyes, the slim nose that flares into wide nostrils, and the broad mouth. The two tusks that frame his face.

I reach out ever so slightly, and he leans his head away from me like I might attack him. Instead, I let my hand land on one of his tusks. He stops moving completely.

"Thank you," I say, and then turn away and run as fast as I possibly can.

CHAPTER 3

RAZ'JIN

No one knows it was me who freed her last night. The town simply wakes up the next morning to find the ropes cut, and the human gone.

There's a little melancholy around the assembled orcs—they were looking forward to letting her rot up there, probably until she died—but they quickly forget about it and move on.

I, on the other hand, am nursing a fierce hangover. I haven't forgotten what I did.

Why I did it... I still can't quite guess. I want to claim it was the alcohol. She tried to kill me first. She tricked me to get away. I should have wanted her dead, too.

But part of me admires her fearlessness, her quick thinking, even the little scar on the side of her face from some battle she barely won. Not to mention that one tantalizing breast hanging out for everyone to see. I wanted to put my hand on it. I should have, last night, when I cut her down from the post.

Maybe I helped her because I couldn't imagine anyone else seeing it but me.

After watching her sprint away into the night, I'd gone back to my room with a huge boner and spent the next thirty minutes dragging my hand from the base to the tip of my cock and back, picturing that perfectly round, petite, pale breast with the pink nipple. In my drunken haze, I wondered what it would taste like. What would she smell like? A pretty thing like that, a human, no less... She'd taste like fruit. She'd smell like flowers and perfume.

I wanted to know the answer, but I know I never will. So I fantasized and fantasized until I ejaculated all over my hand.

If I *could* have her, would I come all over her belly like I do with the trollesses I've fucked? Or would I jam it deep inside her instead and fill up her tiny little hole? My cock was already hard again, so I brought my hand back down to it, and went for round two.

That morning, Blizzek is waiting impatiently for me as I finally make my way to the gate on the edge of town. His eyes are narrow and suspicious.

"Somebody let the little human go," he says. "Ropes were sliced clean off. She couldn't have done that herself."

"How do you know? She was a pretty clever thing."

But my friend isn't that big of an idiot. He just nods and says, "Uh huh."

Despite my raging headache, I suggest we head somewhere new, and see what else we can find. There might be a vein closer to the surface. There's still a chance for us to strike it rich in the Sandteeth.

I wonder if that little human is still around somewhere, or if she's run back home yet. The way she wrapped her hand around my tusk and looked right into my eyes...

If I see her again, I don't think I could control myself.

TELISE

I barely made it out alive, and it's only thanks to him.

I wonder what his name was. At the very least I should have asked that when he cut me down, but I wanted to escape before he changed his mind about helping me—and before something else happened that I can't quite bring myself to imagine.

When he looked at me like that, eating up my half-naked body, I'd felt something new. I wanted him to keep looking. When he cut me down, I expected him to pick me up and drag me away to some cave to take the rest of my clothes off. What would I have done then? Would I have screamed for help, or let him do it?

I'm bruised and cut open in a few places, so after I've sprinted through the darkness for a good few miles to put some distance between myself and the orc town, I have to stop to rest. It's going to be a long trek back to the city, where I hadn't planned on returning so soon. It's a good thirty miles through hotly contested territory, and I have to hope I don't run into any more trollkin on the way. They won't be so merciful when they see an injured, half-naked human on the road, I know that much. I got lucky that the big blue troll took mercy on me, even after I'd nearly knocked him out cold with my foot.

After bandaging up my wounds as best I can at my tiny camp and getting some troubled sleep, I'm ready to continue on. I keep to the brush, hoping that none of these cuts get infected in the meantime.

My leopard got away this time, but I'll try again like I always do. A girl's got to eat after all.

When I finally drag myself into the high walls of the city, I feel like I've had the tar beaten out of me. I see a healer right away, who *tsks* over my stained, dirty bandages and fixes me up with some salve. Once I'm freshly cleaned up and bandaged again, I visit the tailor, where buying a new shirt and pair of pants wipes out what coin I have left.

I have one penny left, just enough to send a letter to Deleran. I'm going to need help getting home and he's the only one I can trust to loan me a little money.

This time, when I go on the hunt, I head to the south instead of the north. I don't want to risk seeing the troll again just in case he's decided he wants a rematch.

RAZ'JIN

After a few weeks, I try to forget about my little run-in with the human. Somehow that disgusting, backward race produced this pretty little creature with eyes like jade fire, and though she doesn't cross my thoughts much during the day, the night-time is a different story.

That's when I imagine how she might feel, with that perfectly soft skin underneath my rough hands. I'd grab that nipple with all four of my fingers and manhandle it, then maybe I'd suckle her like a just-born whelp, too.

But that's not the best part of the fantasy. The best part is when I pull out my drooling cock and start to push it inside her. That's when my hand starts to move faster, my seed already dribbling down the front and lubricating my fingers. I imagine that instead of my hand, it's her tiny little hole squeezing me tight as I thrust in and out. What would she sound like as I pounded her into the ground? I remember the way she shouted at me when she had her knife pointed at my throat and try to bring that noise to the forefront again.

After all this time obsessing over her, imagining how fucking her would feel, I know that I wouldn't pull out at the end. No, I'd let myself release inside her, filling her to the brim until it's spilling out of her. It would coat her small, powerful thighs, dripping out of her as she manages to get back to her feet, and I crush her mouth against mine.

Damn, I guess I was lying. I've really let her into my brain and now she's trapped there, a torturous little thought banging against the walls holding it inside.

Blizzek gives me a puzzled look as we extract another penny-sized chunk of gold. We did hit it big, after all—big enough that I'll be able to take a few months off after this trip. I should be thrilled about it, but instead, I'm lost in my thoughts.

"I thought you'd be happier," he says, tossing another tiny nugget into our bag. We'll split the profit fifty-fifty after taxes. Fucking taxes, heading straight up the pole to our idiot Grand Chieftain, sitting atop his throne of hides and teeth. "We hit a good one."

"Yeah, it's great," I say absently, chiseling out another little piece. It's difficult work, though, and my hands are finally starting to get tired.

"Get your head in the game, Raz. I can't have my partner dozing off on the job."

With a sigh, I try to refocus. I've got to stop thinking about the human with the pale skin and perfect breasts. "Right."

"Thanks," Blizzek says. "You're never going to see her again, so stop thinking about it."

I know that he's right, and I don't think I like it. But this is the way it should be.

I'm a troll, and she's not. We can't even speak the same

language. It could never happen the way it happens in my imagination, I know that for sure. So I try to push her out of my mind and get on with my work, pledging to find some good cunt next time I'm in the big city and finally forget about her.

TELISE

"I'm sorry, you *what?*" Deleran tosses back some wine. He lent me some money to get back home after I finished up my hunt. "I can't believe you'd let your guard down long enough to get captured."

"I was a little distracted."

"Right, you tried to take out two trollkin alone and almost got your ass whooped." He narrows his eyes. "And then you, what, kissed him? On his big ugly mug?"

"It wasn't that ugly," I say reflexively. Deleran scowls even deeper. "It got me out of the situation intact, didn't it?"

"I'm sure there are other ways you could've gone about it."

But I don't care what he thinks. It worked. And I even liked it, just a little bit.

"You know," he says after another swig. "You've always been kind of a freak, Telise. So somehow shocked, but also not surprised."

"He's the only reason I'm not dead right now," I say. "I could be just a sack of bones hanging from a post."

Deleran doesn't respond right away. "Yeah," he finally says, staring down into his cup. "I am glad you're still alive, even if it's only because you kissed a damn trollkin right on the mouth. He must have a crush on you now."

Without my permission, my heart jumps a little. What if he

does? While I've been revisiting the moment that I kissed him over and over, has he been thinking about me, too?

"You didn't realize?" Deleran asks, noting my surprise. "The troll only let you go because it has a thing for you now."

Huh. Why does that tickle me in a place deep down? I like the idea of him desiring me. I wonder if kissing him sent off a whole chain reaction of events in his mind.

"Guess it's a good thing I did what I did, isn't it?" I grin at him. "It was even a little hot."

Deleran's face turns red. "You have to be joking." He shakes his head in deep disapproval. "Telise, I can't wrap my mind around you."

"Guess I am a freak."

Deleran did help me and my leopard hide get home safely, so I owe it to him to be a little nice.

"Did you get some good ass while I was gone?" I ask.

"It was all right." But it doesn't look like his heart is in it.

"I made you something." I had the whole trip back on the ship to do some arts and crafts. I pull out a pair of boots, the ankles rimmed with generic rabbit fur, and set them on the table in front of him.

His eyes light up. He grabs the boots and holds them up, evaluating the shape of the foot, studying my stitch work. If I know anything about my best friend, it's that he appreciates fashion. And these boots are fashion.

"For me?" He immediately rips off his shoes and puts the new boots on. "Wow. Lined, too?"

"Can't have you freezing or anything." Winter is approaching soon, and I plan on staying on my feet. I hope that he'll come with me—I'm a little more wary of traveling alone now.

"Are you dragging me up north?" he asks, now obviously impatient with me. "Is this a bribe?"

"It's a gift!" I do my best to appear put out by his accusation. But Deleran simply doesn't speak, giving me a *stop lying to my face* look instead. "I want to get some bear, okay? People are all about bear right now. And beaver. There's only one place I can get that."

With a dramatic sigh, Deleran drops his head to the table. "I should never have left Great Oak with you."

"Didn't think you'd get dragged all over the world, huh?" I smile. "We'll go by train. I hear the trip is lovely."

CHAPTER 4

RAZ'JIN

Finally, we're back in civilization. I usually don't mind the isolation of life as a prospector but roughing it does get old after a while. I wouldn't mind a beer, a meal, and a soft bed once we sell off our gold.

I've forgotten how smelly this place can get, though. Unwashed trollkin of all kinds, with all their various foods and farm animals, stink up the streets and alleyways. There's not much sense to the organization of Kalishagg, but you learn your way around eventually. It started as a single troll settlement and expanded upon itself from there, one clay building and sagging tent at a time.

We find our guy's shop up on the second level, across a rickety wooden bridge. Old Magna's shop is exactly the same as the previous dozen times I've visited with a bag full of unprocessed, raw ore.

"Only 560?" Blizzek is incensed by Magna's price after he weighs it.

"Sorry," he says. "The value of gold has gone down. You'd have been better off with silver."

Blizzek looks like he's about to tear out his hair, so I quickly grab him by the shoulder and wheel him out of the shop. "We should just take it," I hiss. "We're lucky anyone's buying at all right now." There's a war going on out there, and gold is in far lower demand than iron and copper.

"Fine." He pushes me away. "Make it 600, Magna, and we're gold."

The old man sighs at him. Blizzek's jokes make me want to throw up. "580, final offer."

It's easy enough to split two ways. Magna collects the tax and we're done.

Neither of us has to say what we're thinking once we leave the shop. It's time to spend some coin—but not so much that we get robbed in our sleep, of course.

We don't go to the brothel right away. That's a last-ditch effort if picking up women at the bar doesn't work out. I buy a new set of shoulder cuffs with steel tips, which look both stylish and expensive. That's what a trolless wants, after all: Somebody with big shoulders and money to spend.

It doesn't take us long to get called over to a table with two trollesses and an orcess. They're clearly out on the prowl, too, and soon the two troll women are giving each other elbows and snarls as they figure out which one's going to go upstairs with me.

"There's no need to fight," I say, setting down two fresh beers. I put a hand on each of their shoulders. "I'm amenable to a group event. I have plenty to give." They both look at my crotch, where my cock is already growing pretty warm and fat for them under my new leather pants. The trollesses exchange smirks, and then we're off to the races.

As I tear the first one's clothes off and bury myself inside her, then pull the other one close so I can finger her, I should be thrilled. It's a two-for-the-price-of-one deal. The first trolless moans under me as I ride her, but for some reason, I just can't feel the same enthusiasm. I bring the other troll woman up to my face and suck on her as hard as I can, then we swap. The first trolless comes all over my mouth, and I find I don't like the taste of it. I push her away quickly and reach my orgasm inside the other one, then pull myself out and gush all over her back.

They want to cuddle up afterwards, but I just want to get the stench of them off of me, so I open the door and indignant, they both stomp out. Once they're gone, I draw the water and sit in a cold bath, trying to clean my cock off as best I can.

I stay there for a long time, trying to understand what went wrong. I've always liked getting my dick a bit dirty. And two at once? A very rare treat. But something about it all felt strange —off, like meat when it's just starting to go bad.

I snarl and push my wet hair out of my eyes. I know whose fault this is, and I wish I had just let her die there. But now she's stuck inside me, and I don't know how to claw her out.

TELISE

It's a good winter, if winters can be good. After the sale of my Wicke's Leopard cloak, I buy two train tickets for Deleran and I to head north. He grumbles the entire way, and then continues grumbling as I drag him through snow drifts and across frozen lakes. But I'm hot on the trail of a great male bear with perfect gray fur and a few classy stripes of white. I was going to shoot for boot lining, but this bear's just so pretty, I might turn him into a rich lady's centerpiece.

But Deleran tolerates all of it. One particularly cold night, we're curled up in our furs with the sled blocking us from the wind, and I feel a little breath of air enter my cocoon.

"Ugh." I move to push it back down, because all I want is a bit of rest in the middle of this storm, but I find someone's hand there instead.

It's Deleran, and he's crawling into my bed.

I don't react at first, because I have no idea how to react. He lifts the blanket up so he can slide inside, and it's only once we're face-to-face that I think to push him away.

"What are you doing?" I ask. He's letting in all the cold air. But I know the answer to that question before I even ask it, because my childhood best friend is pressed up against me with a raging hard-on.

Ugh. Disgusting.

"It's cold," he says, acting surprised that I've put some distance between us. "I thought you might want to warm up."

"That's not what you're after. Don't play fucking coy with me."

This seems to land, because Deleran withdraws his hands from me.

"I don't get you." He puts a few inches between us but doesn't move away. "You know women would fall over them-selves to do this with me."

I give him a hard shove this time, and he rolls out of my bed with surprise. Then I close up the furs around me tight again and turn away so we don't have to look at each other.

"I don't like you that way," I say, now feeling cross and strangely hurt. I'd always felt safe around him, like I wouldn't ever have to worry about this. But now it's out there, and I do.

He doesn't speak for a while. Then, after a while he says, "I'm sorry, Tea." It's the old nickname he called me when we were younger. "I'm cold and horny and..." Deleran clears his throat. "And you're gorgeous, and I really like you."

He what? I'm what?

I curl up tighter around myself. This is information I didn't want—information I didn't need. Nothing will ever be right and the same between us now that I know it.

"I don't feel at all the same way about you," I say.

"Oof." He groans like I've stabbed him. "You couldn't have at least tried to soften the blow?"

"No." I'm scowling at nobody. "I needed to make sure it's out there in no uncertain terms."

We both fall silent after that. It'll be a while before I can fall asleep again, because now I'm worried about Deleran slipping into my bed. I know he wouldn't, not after turning him down with such brutality, but the thought is there.

"Is this about the goddamned troll?" he asks suddenly. He sits up in his furs, the heavy wind buffeting his hair. "You won't sleep with me because you kissed a troll?"

"It has nothing to do with that." Okay, maybe it does have a tiny bit to do with that, but also not at all. "I'm not interested. That's all you need to know."

He sighs, defeated, and returns to his bed. Now there's really no more talking.

The next day, he tries to pretend like everything is normal again—joking around, bitching when I ask him to build the fire, even making fun of my aim when I miss a rabbit—but nothing feels the same. Not anymore.

By the time we head back to civilization, we're hardly speaking to each other. The train ride is long.

"I shouldn't have ever done it," Deleran says, leaned back against his seat. He lets out a deep, weary sigh. "I fucked it all up."

"You sort of did." But at least him acknowledging it, and then beating himself up about it, brings me a little smile.

"Can you please forgive me, Tea?" The train is slowing

down, pulling into the station. "Can you forget it ever happened?"

"I can't forget, but I can forgive."

"That's the most I can ask for, I guess."

I hold out a hand, and he takes it. We shake.

Maybe that troll really did ruin me.

RAZ'JIN

I don't fuck anymore trollesses, and Blizzek is concerned about me. I turn them down when they approach us in bars—he doesn't, of course.

"What's gotten into you?" he asks, sounding like an annoyed parent with a pouting child.

But I don't have an answer he would like. How can I tell him that I don't even desire my own kind anymore? That's a fucked-up thing to say out loud. I was ruined by one tiny, pinkish tit, one small kiss on the mouth, and a delicate hand on my tusk.

After months pass like this, I'm the one who makes the stupid suggestion that we head to the Frattern Islands. There have always been rumors you can find beautiful emeralds there, coming up from under the waves. While the grunts go out there and die in the war, the nobility are sitting pretty, and they want equally pretty jewels to give all their many wives. And I will be the one to provide them.

"Emeralds?" Blizzek squints at me. "We're going into contested territory for... emeralds?"

He won't connect the dots, I'm sure. But all I want is to see those fierce green eyes again, even if they're just peering up at me from the sand. Not to mention that contested territory—

where neither trollkin nor humans have complete control of the landscape—gives me the slightest, slimmest of chances of seeing her again.

"I can go by myself," I say, huffing.

"Fine." Blizzek just shrugs, then rolls his shoulders. "I've got enough money in the bank. I don't need to be fishing for emeralds where there certainly aren't any."

Great. The perfect opportunity to wander off on my own and see what becomes of me. Prospecting is all I have now that pleasures of the body are off the table. The only two things a troll desires are women and money. If I can't have one, at least I'll have the other.

"I'll see you in a few months, then."

It's a long trip by ship from Kalishagg to the islands off the coast, and it's not really the best time of year, anyway. They're not tropical islands, not by any stretch of the imagination. They're the kind with deep-inset rocky shores and high cliffs buffeted by great, frigid waves.

Blizzek gives me a confused goodbye as I pack up my bag and head for the caravan. It'll take me to the port, where I'll hop on a ship to carry me across the water. It's a few weeks each way, and who knows how long I'll spend searching for treasure?

"Don't do anything stupid," he says as I depart.

"What constitutes 'stupid'?" I ask.

"You know what I mean."

Maybe I'm not as slick as I've thought, and Blizzek has caught onto me. I just pretend to be perplexed by his answer, and then I'm off to find my fortune across the sea.

Chapter 5

Telise

The letter was waiting for me at the courier's office when I returned to the capital.

"I learned of your name while complimenting a man's leopard-hide cloak," it reads. "I've been searching for a new apprentice to share my trade, and I think that perhaps you would be the one."

An apprentice? I've been an amateur for who knows how many years, and in that time, I've picked up on my own most of what an apprentice would have learned. But it's signed by a name I recognize: Sden Noralt, an artisan who works out of the neutral city of Eyra Cove. It's on the edge of the Frattern Islands, a highly contested territory where fighting frequently breaks out.

A brave and a foolish place to run a business, but with twice as many potential customers.

What reason do I have to refuse it? I don't think I want to

travel with Deleran again, and I don't have any other grand ideas now that I've cleaned, stitched, sewn, and sold my bear pelts.

"All right," I write back. "I'm in." And I get on a boat before he can answer.

It costs me a pretty penny to get there, and I have to carry all of my heavy equipment with me, so I pay for an extra-large room on the ship. But I have a sense that this is the right move, and that if I follow through, something significant in my life will change. And that's just what I need right now.

Eyra Cove is a bustling, somewhat terrifying place. Everything is in motion all the time, from the piers where a significant amount of the business is done, all the way to the hopping inns and bars and various other hedonistic holes. You can find anything you want in Eyra Cove—and do anything you want, too. It's just the sort of place for me.

Sden works out of a respectable establishment, and I like him right away. He's all human through-and-through, but with none of the hang-ups. He barters in Freysian with humans, and switches seamlessly to Trollkin to sell a pair of gloves to an orc. No one seems to bat an eyelash at his prices, either. Every piece he makes is branded with his mark.

"That cloak you made was one of the prettiest I've seen," Sden says when I finally arrive, dragging my piles of gear along with me. "You have a lot of talent, but I can see you've never been classically trained."

"Is it that obvious?" I say.

"Not to most. But I think we can clean you up good, and you could become a master craftsman someday, too."

That's a high honor. I could charge double, even triple what I do now for my better pieces with a master craftsman license.

"And you're doing this for me because...?"

"Well, I'll take a cut of all your profits while you work under me," he says. "And you'll work—supervised—on some of my pieces without pay. That's the trade."

Hmm. It doesn't feel very fair, but I'll be learning a skill that's priceless. So I accept his offer, and we shake on it.

"Very good." Without another word, he gestures to his back room. "Why don't you get to work?"

I don't need to be told twice.

A good portion of my money will go towards renting out a room at the inn, which is unfortunate. I won't get to save nearly as much as I would've liked, thinking that surely my new master would put me up.

But I've also underestimated how much money one can make with a storefront in Eyra Cove. I sell almost all of the pieces I've brought with me within a few days.

"I can tell that fur is your specialty," Sden says one day, and unveils a whole pallet of furs in need of attention. "One of my hunters brought this in."

"I won't need to hunt my own pelts anymore?" I ask. I'm almost disappointed to hear this—hunting and collecting is one of the things I've always enjoyed about this trade.

"No. Your focus will be entirely on craft." He'll take a bigger cut of pieces I sell made with them, but I expected that.

So I take up residence in the inn, and for months, I work myself nearly to the bone at Sden's shop. I start to pick up a few words of Trollkin here and there. It's bizarre to shake hands with orcs as we strike deals. I know how to count, at least, which makes it far easier to bargain and haggle with our customers.

Every once in a while, some fight will break out between a drunk human and an equally drunk troll, but it's always handled quickly, efficiently, and usually with some blood. Security is no joke around Eyra Cove.

But it's a lonely place, too. Sden is a quiet, harsh man who works almost entirely in silence, and everyone else is a passer-by. Even though I've drowned myself in my work, I'm starving in places I haven't ever felt before.

I need companionship, friendship, or something else that feels just out of my reach.

RAZ'JIN

Maybe the emeralds were a lie.

I spend days, and then weeks, searching the islands for any sign of a green flash. Blizzek's little ore-tracking device wouldn't help me here, anyway. That's what makes jewels such a pain in the ass to prospect—there's really no way to find them without sheer luck.

I lie underneath my tarp, trying to wait out the rain for what feels like hours. I'm just about to give up and go home, when I notice the rain is forcing the sand to recede. I jump out of my tarp and start wandering the shore as the sand pulls away from the rocks, draining off into the sea. Then I find it: There's a small, glimmering emerald, buried inside a great boulder. I kneel by it and pull out my pickaxe.

Here it is. The jewel I came looking for.

But when I have it out and in my palms, I don't feel the way I'd hoped. It doesn't trigger some big change, like I think I'd been expecting. It's just a pretty rock sitting in my hand. An expensive rock, for sure, but a rock, nonetheless.

I stuff it into my pocket and return to my tarp. After

making a light meal out of a turtle, I rip the tarp down and bundle it all up, then trudge through the rain back the way I came.

I'll head to Eyra Cove and get on the next ship home, then sell the emerald off in Kalishagg. I can't stand this anymore, whatever it is—this obnoxious funk I've found myself in. I'm about ready to bash my own head in. Maybe what I really need is to join the war effort. I could dress myself up in some nice armor, take my double-handed axe, and kill some human scum. Maybe some good, old-fashioned bloodshed would soothe me in the place I'm desperately needing to be soothed.

When I reach the city, it's less busy than when I arrived. The cool winds of winter are blowing in, and most people who aren't idiots have gone back home by now. But there are still locals around, and a few like me trying to eke out a living before retiring home for the coming months.

I turn the emerald over inside my hand as I browse the shops. It reminds me of one of her bright green eyes, shining out of that pale, freckled face. So I buy my room for the night with some of my few remaining coins, and head downstairs to have a drink.

The inn is quiet, only one argument breaking out near the fire pit between a human and an orc. What it's about, I can't imagine, but it gets quickly diffused. The human is kicked out on his ass, and I have to laugh a little at that.

It's growing late and I'm about to head to my room to retire for the night when the door is roughly kicked open. A small person in a thick, fur-trim hood and stylish matching pants walks in. I can tell without trying that it's a human female, with good, thick hips. Immediately I wonder what she looks like under there.

Ugh. Here I go again. Maybe coming to neutral territory

wasn't such a good idea now that I seem to have a penchant for women that are totally off-limits to me.

I turn away as she approaches the bar and sits four seats down from me. I don't need to look at her. In fact, I should probably set aside this last half of my beer and just leave now, before I get any stupid ideas.

I'm getting up and dropping a coin on the bar when I accidentally glance down at my neighbor. She's pulled her hood off, and underneath, she has a whole waterfall of red-orange hair. There's a nick across her freckled cheek that I instantly recognize.

It's her.

I must make some sort of gagging noise in my surprise because she immediately turns her head to look at me. The very same recognition that I had dawns on her face, and I think that for sure she's going to get up and run the fuck away, as fast as she can.

Instead, something very different happens. She takes in the sight of me, all of me, and smiles.

TELISE

He's here.

The trollkin I met in the woods that day, who cut me down and helped me escape certain death, is sitting right next to me at a bar in Eyra Cove.

I thought for sure I'd never, ever see him again. It would be like finding a needle in a whole field full of haystacks. And yet here he is, all seven feet of him, getting up out of his seat with half of a full beer in front of him.

His blue skin looks more sallow than I remember, and I'm

shocked at how clear my memory of him is in comparison to seeing him now. Even though he seems tired, he has that same carefree posture and the hunch to his shoulders that says he doesn't worry about much of anything besides his coin. His tusks are more scratched up since last time, like he's used them a few times to protect his face from an incoming attack.

But those clear, clever eyes are the same. I would recognize them anywhere.

I can't help smiling when I see him. If only I could have thanked him for freeing me that night, I would have. I was terrified, though, and wanted nothing more than to see that miserable orcish town fade into the distance.

He is so stunned at seeing me that he freezes in place. So he recognizes me, too. Good. I did leave an impression on him just like he left one on me.

"Hi," I say in Freysian, and then quickly realize he won't understand me. I try again in Trollkin. "Hello."

He blinks a few times. The shock runs deeper than I expected.

"Hello," he says back in Trollkin. I find his hand has dropped to the little hatchet at his belt, and my smile turns into a frown.

Does he want to kill me, after all this time?

I lift both my hands up in surrender. "No worries," I say in Trollkin. I turn back to the bar right as my beer arrives and tear my eyes away from him. Clearly, he's not as excited to see me as I am to see him. I'll just pretend it didn't happen.

That's when I feel the bar shift, and the huge troll takes a seat right next to me.

"Hello," he says again. "It's you."

I don't know if that's exactly what he's saying, but I do know *you*, and by his tone of voice I'm pretty sure that's what he means. The bartender watches us out of the corner of his eye, as if expecting a fight to break out.

"It is me," I say, trying to imitate his grammar. His eyes squint a little, and the sides of his mouth turn up. He has such a wide, almost pretty mouth, pulled back where his big tusks emerge from it. They're really just big teeth, or so I learned from a book. Not much different than my own canines.

He laughs then, and I realize I must have said something wrong. He corrects me in Trollkin, and I repeat it back to him. He gives me a faint nod of approval.

"I'm Telise," I say, planting my hand over my heart.

"Tell-issa." His mouth tries to wrap around the word but can't quite do it.

"Tel-eese," I say.

"Tel-eesa." He repeats it back to me, a little bit better this time, but not quite there. Good enough.

"Who are you?" I ask in Trollkin. I know that much, at least.

He places his hand on his chest, imitating what I just did. "Raz'jin."

That's a good one. It fits him and his head of untamed hair. It's sticking out all over, and I just want to go up behind him and fix it.

"Raz'jin," I repeat back to him. He makes an impressed face and nods.

"Good," he says.

"Thank you."

My time here learning how to negotiate in Trollkin is really paying dividends right now. That's when I realize I still need to thank him.

"That time," I say, not sure how to put into words what I want to get across. I hold my hands up and pretend they're bound tight, then imitate cutting through one. "You did?"

Raz'jin nods. "Yes."

I smile again. "Thank you."

His eyes widen at this. They're orange all over, no irises to be seen, and they're streaked through with a red that's almost the color of my hair.

"You're welcome, Tel-eesa."

Almost there.

I don't know much else in Trollkin, so I take a long swig of my beer and wait for him to say something, instead. But when I look up again, I find his eyes are riveted on my face, not a single word coming out of his mouth.

"What?" I ask.

As if I've startled him out of a dream, Raz'jin shakes his head. "Nothing." He takes another sip of his own beer, and the awkward silence falls again.

I wish I knew what to do. There's so much I want to know about him, but I'm not sure how to ask. "Where from?" I finally say. I've taken him by surprise a third time with my question.

"Argsul," he answers. I roughly know where that is—it's firmly within the Trollkin lands. I nod in understanding. "You?"

"Great Oak," I say.

He tilts his head. "West?"

I nod. He *hmms*. "No trollkin there. Safe."

Very much unlike the world I live in now.

Raz'jin puts two coins on the bar this time, and calls something out to the orcish bartender I can't understand. The bartender gives Raz'jin an equally confused look, but when the troll hits the bar with his fist, the bartender gets working.

He sure knows how to get his way.

Soon, there are two more beers in front of us: One for me and one for him. It's such a polite gesture, that I smile again and say, "Thank you."

We each lift our beers up by the handle, and Raz'jin holds his out towards me. He wants to cheers.

We tap our mugs.

"Cheers," he says in Trollkin.

"Cheers," I say in Freysian. And then, he smiles back, and takes a long drink.

CHAPTER 6

RAZ'JIN

That smile was like magic.

I've never had a human smile at me before. Between her pink lips, Tel-eesa has bright white teeth, all as straight as they get. And it's a pretty name, to boot.

She even speaks some Trollkin now. That was a fascinating surprise. Along with the part where she didn't run away from me. No—she asked me questions. She thanked me for freeing her that night and saving her life. The bartender keeps looking at us curiously, until I shoot him a deadly glare and he pivots away.

I don't know what to make of it, really. The human is smiling and nodding like we've been friends for a long time. Her hair is longer now, and tumbles down the sides of her face in waves that reflect the lamplight. I take in every inch of her, from those shining green eyes, down to the delicately exposed skin at her throat. Her outfit is fancy, well-tailored, and I wonder if she's gotten rich since the last time we met.

While she asks me about where I'm from, I can't help looking, studying the way her jerkin wraps around her pert breasts, how it tightens at her waist and flares into a fur cuff at her hips.

I'm not sure why I buy her a beer. I feel like I need to impress her.

"Cheers," she says.

"Cheers."

We each take a drink, and when I'm finished with mine, I'm not sure what to say next. I know what I'm feeling deep inside, of course. Every inch of my coarse body is longing for her. I could simply eat her in one big mouthful. I want to tear that pretty coat off of her and see what's underneath. Is the hair between her legs as bright and red as the hair on her head? I want to know what her legs look like, her arms, her feet. Her hands are tiny and delicate, and they almost can't wrap all the way around the handle of her beer mug.

Instantly I imagine that same hand wrapped around me, moving from the base of my cock up to the tip and back again. I almost choke on my words.

"What are you doing here?" I ask her in Trollkin.

She squints thoughtfully, trying to parse through what I'm asking.

So I try again, with something a little simpler. "Why here?" I gesture at the inn around us.

This clicks. Tel-eesa picks up the hood of her coat and unclasps it from around her neck. She draws the coat off of her shoulders and now I can get a much better look at her. Her shoulders are strong, but still feminine. Her neck is long and slender. She's not tall for a human, I don't think.

She holds out the cloak to me. Is she offering it? It would never fit.

"I make," she says as I finally take the cloak from her. I feel the soft fur, the carefully pounded leather. It's all pliable under my hands.

She made this?

"Wow." I examine the whole thing. It's well-crafted, and certainly nicer than anything I've ever owned. "Beautiful."

This earns an even bigger smile, and I pass the cloak back to her. So she's here making wares to be sold. It's a smart—and bold—idea to set up shop in Eyra Cove. That explains the smattering of Trollkin she's learned.

"Thank you," she says. She doesn't put it back on, and I certainly don't mind. I can barely keep my eyes off of her. I'm removing each of her garments in my mind, working my way down her body to her feet. They would be such petite feet, with five whole toes each. I would bring them into my mouth and suck on them if I could.

"Why you here?" she asks.

Oh. Right. My ridiculous quest for the green jewels.

A big emerald like the one I found could fetch me more than the gold did. I don't want anyone to know I have it, because that's how you get stabbed and robbed in your sleep. But at the same time, I want to continue this conversation with her. And I want to see how wide her green eyes get when she sees it.

I hold up a finger to my lips, gesturing for her to keep quiet. Her eyebrows draw together in confusion as I reach down into my pocket and draw it out.

The emerald. It glitters in the low light of the inn. Her mouth drops open, but before she can make a sound, she covers it with one hand. I can tell she wants to reach towards the jewel, to run her fingers over it... And I think of Blizzek saying, *Don't do anything stupid.*

But I let her touch it anyway.

Not only that, I allow her to sweep it up into her small

hands. It's large, I realize—filling up most of her palm. She keeps it hidden under the bar top as she surveys it, admires it. Her eyes are wide and filled with wonder.

Then, slowly, she slips it back to me. Her fingers linger on mine for a long time. They're so small in comparison, I could swallow up both of her hands in just one of mine.

I'm already aching for her.

I slide the emerald back into my pocket and take a big swallow of my beer. I can feel it rising into my head, shifting my thoughts around and garbling them. My hands are burning where she touched me, and now I want nothing more than for her to touch me again.

"Very good," she says, and I think it's because those are the only words she has for what she really wants to say. But her eyes say it for her. "Beautiful."

I'm not sure how much more I can take. The longer I look at her, the more blood starts to rush down to my groin, filling me up. I'm simply glad for my thick pants and the leather coil I have wrapped around my waist.

"Thank you."

Tel-eesa pulls out a little bag and makes a gesture like she's filling it with coins. This makes me smile. She thinks that surely it will make me rich.

I shake my head. "Some," I say. "Not much."

She makes a frowny face. It's really quite cute. There's even more blood flowing downward now, and it's making sitting this way uncomfortable.

What am I doing right now? I'm flirting with a human woman at a bar. It's ridiculous in so many different ways. And what's really baffling me is how much I'm enjoying myself.

I suddenly feel like I need to escape, because if I don't, I'm going to grab her arm and pull her against me, and then seize her mouth in mine. I'm going to drag her upstairs with me and rip off all of her clothes, and then—

It's almost like she can see what's happening on my face, because with the utmost caution, she reaches out and puts her hand on my leg.

I suck in a sharp breath of air. Her fingers are nearly searing me through the leather. When I look down, her green eyes have darkened to the color of a winter forest. Her mouth is no longer smiling. There's something else on her face, something I can't even let myself interpret.

So I reach down and put my hand over hers.

TELISE

He's hot. Boiling hot. His fingers clasp around mine, and my hand disappears into his.

I'm worried that I'm being too forward with what I want, when I'm still not even sure I want it. But that part of me way deep down that has been hungering for who knows how long... It's drooling now.

You're a freak, Telise. Was Deleran right? Am I attracted to a troll?

But why not? He's tall, and filled with muscle, and handsome to boot. Maybe it's not a face to everyone's taste, but it sure is mine. And the tusks that veer off to either side of his mouth? Perfect for grabbing onto. I could yank him down to my height again and kiss him just like I did the first time we met, when I had a dagger at his throat.

I'm glad he doesn't hold that against me now.

Slowly, never taking his eyes off of me, Raz'jin starts to guide my hand up his leg. I go along with it. He pulls my fingers under the coil and there, I can feel it. He's hard underneath, like a solid rock.

I try not to jerk my hand away in surprise, because I wouldn't want to think I'm repelled by it. It's just not what I expected; something I didn't know I wanted until right now.

Tentatively I reach out and let my fingers trail along the lump in his pants. I look up at his face, and his eyes are focused intently on me, something dark and thirsty lying behind them.

Once I've reached the tip of him, I move my fingers back again, all the way under the leather coil. He sucks in a breath and then, more fiercely than I expected, he grabs my hand in his. He shoves it hard against the cock that I already know is throbbing underneath there. A burst of heat races down my chest to the crux between my legs.

I know what he wants now. And if I get alone with him, I know what he's going to do. Do I want that, too? Do I want this creature to throw me down and tear my clothes off, and then pull out this enormous beast and shove it inside me?

A tingle darts all the way up my spine. The hungry part of me says, *Yes, of course that's what I want.* While the rational part of me says, *But he's a monster.*

I grip his lump hard, the same way he's shoving down on my hand, and he gasps. I can see over the bar top as the bartender looks up again, and his mouth falls slack when he registers what's happening.

I remove my hand quickly. Raz'jin's eyes flick open and look at me with disappointment—until I grab onto one of his huge fingers in my hand and pull, then point upstairs. His ears flick forward, and his eyes grow wide.

He grabs my entire hand and pulls me off the bar stool. I remember at the last moment to grab my cloak, and he drags me through the inn almost faster than I can keep up. Every single head turns to watch us go past, and I know my face is a fiery red as we finally reach the stairs.

Everything is happening in slow motion when he reaches down and picks me up without any effort at all. I half expect him to throw me over his shoulder like a sack of potatoes the way he takes the steps two at a time, until we're up on my floor.

I point up ahead. "That one." I know this phrase well. With a sharp nod he crosses to the door and sets me down in front of it. I pull out my key, and my hands are shaking. Why am I shaking? Am I scared, or happy, or something else entirely?

Finally the door is open and Raz'jin shoves it wide, and I scurry inside ahead of him. He closes it with an audible slam, and I can tell then he's hungry.

Ravenous.

For me.

I'm almost certain that he's going to eat me up, swallow me whole and spit out my bones, like in an old painting. And I'm already so wet for him.

I expect him to shove me down on the bed when he approaches, but he stops abruptly in front of me, then leans down. He puts one hand under my chin and brings me close to his face.

This time, Raz'jin is the one who kisses me. And it's no surprise peck on the lips—it's an invasion. His mouth pulls me in, and his hand drops to my ass. He squeezes it, hard, feeling out the roundness of it with his four large fingers. A few guttural words fall out of his mouth, but I can make out one of them:

"Want."

Suddenly I'm desiring nothing more than his hands on the rest of me. I grab his tusk, just like I did that very first time, and pull him towards me until I'm falling back on the bed and taking him down with me.

Raz'jin's mouth never releases mine as his fingers explore me. He shoves his waist hard against me so I can feel the huge lump under his pants between my legs. I lift my hips and grind them against him, showing him how much I want it.

Finally, he lets my mouth go, and he's panting as hard as I am. He doesn't need words to say what he's after.

I don't want him to rip off my any of my nice clothes, so I slowly back away from him. Reluctantly, Raz'jin lets me go, and I unbutton my jerkin. When it falls off, the look that comes over him is... Something like relief, as if he's seeing a very old friend.

He grabs me around the middle, then seizes one of my breasts in his hand. I worry he's going to be too rough with my nipples, but the moment his fingers reach one they slow down, and I'm surprised by the gingerness with which he takes it in his huge hands. He pushes me back to the bed again and drops his head, taking the same nipple in his mouth. He sucks on it hard, like he's trying to pull milk out of me, and his long tongue traces every part of it.

He says something in Trollkin that I don't understand, and it sounds like a prayer.

Chapter 7

Raz'jin

"I dreamed of these."

And here they are, in the palm of my hand. They're full and round, with the perfectly pert, pink nipples, just like in my fantasy.

I could take her fast. I could tear my pants and hers off right now and find out just how tight she is for me. But that wouldn't be any fun, not when I've been waiting so long for this. That's what I was doing all this time, and I just didn't realize it—waiting. This moment was coming for me someday, like a train barreling down a track. It was inevitable that I would find her again.

No, I want to savor her. Sip her slowly, like a strong drink. I want to make her cream into the palm of my hand, and then smear it all over her and use it to fuck her. It's even better that she wants it hard and fast, because that means she'll be ready for me when it's time.

I have to stop and think twice about that. *She wants me.*

This small creature with hair like sunlight and the biggest eyes I've ever seen wants *me*, just as much as I want her. Unfathomable.

"More," she says, in Trollkin. She's using the "more" for money and not the "more" for sex, but that only makes me chuckle against her breast. I release her, and she's shivering underneath me like a small animal. I just want to shove myself inside her.

"Take these off," I say, gesturing at the pants. I saw how gingerly she took off her jerkin earlier, and I would hate to ruin her good work. Tel-eesa obeys me, pulling the pants off, and revealing the smooth, pale hip and thigh underneath. She does indeed have a mound of brown-red fur just between her legs, and I'm elated to learn this. But before I can press her down to the bed again, she puts a hand on my chest to stop me.

"Yours, now," she says, with a surprisingly stern look. There's no way I can deny her after that. I undo my shoulder pieces, tossing them to the floor. Then goes my leather tunic, my undershirt. She watches me with an intensity I've never seen, like a hunter waiting for its prey to walk into range.

Has this little human been hungering for me as much as I've been for her?

When I pull off the coil, I find her crawling off the bed towards me. She licks her lips, and as soon as I have my pants down past my hips, my cock springs out.

Then her mouth is on me, and it's the last thing I expected —but oh, does she feel good. She starts at the head with her tongue and traces it all the way down me, then back up again, over and over, until she's lathered up the entire surface of me.

And then she puts her lips around me. She can't get it far in —I'm too big for that—but far enough that I'm grunting and groaning against her.

Now that she's warmed me up good, there's only one thing

I want, and that's to be buried inside her. But I try to stop myself and take a breath. She's so small that if I'm not careful, I could break her, and then I couldn't fuck her again and again like I plan to.

Finally I take her shoulders in my hands and pull her away, so she has to stop sucking on me. I'm breathing so hard that it pushes the hair back from her face.

"Lie down," I say, pointing at the bed. She obeys, falling onto her back again. I want to look at her as I make her mine.

Remember, not yet. I try to steady myself and shove down everything my cock wants right now. Instead, I drop my head between her legs. Down there she looks like nothing I've ever seen before—tiny and pink, with the smallest slit I could imagine. There's no way I'll fit in there.

I heft up her legs, her knees over my shoulders, and lean in. All I have to do is reach out with my tongue to touch her and immediately, she cries out, like a little songbird. Her legs seize, but they're trapped by my hands. I lick her again and again, and she responds every time. When I bring my hand up to put a finger inside her, though, I find something I didn't expect.

I can't get it in even an inch. She's so tiny there it's like a pinhole. How is that possible?

Licking harder, I push on it, and her cry of pleasure twists into one of surprise, and then pain. If my finger can't fit inside her, there's no way my cock will, too.

"Keep going," she says when I pause to examine what I'm dealing with. "Keep going."

So I do what I'm told and continue licking her as hard and fast as I can. Slowly, her entrance starts to widen up for me, and it's barely enough to get one finger inside. She gasps and buries her hands in my hair. Soon she's riding my hand and my mouth, every brush of my tongue sending a surge through her little body. I can tell by the rising tenor of her cries that she's almost there, and I move my finger faster and faster, waiting for the moment she bursts like a piece of the most delicious fruit.

There it is—she cries out as she clenches all around me, and the trickle of her juice slips down my hand. I lick it off, and what I taste is everything I could ever have imagined. It's perfect, salty and sweet, and just what I needed.

Now it's time. I nudge her back onto the bed and push her down onto her back. My cock is thirsting for her, shuddering in its readiness. I'm finally going to have her.

I bring two fingers down to her entrance instead, trying to fit both inside her. I need her to be ready, too, for this to work. She recoils a little, and her knees press together. I frown, starting to feel concerned. She's so tight and so small. How is it going to possibly—

Oh.

That's when it hits me. Not only is there a beautiful human lying on a bed in front of me, but she's never invited a male inside her before, either. I'll be her first one.

TELISE

Maybe I should have told him, but how could I? I have no idea what the Trollkin word for "virgin" is. And even if I did, what does it matter? He's going to take me either way. I want him to, more than I've ever wanted anything.

But if Raz'jin's going to be my first, I know how I want it, and it isn't with his fingers.

I pull his hand away from me, and his face shifts in confusion. Then I reach out for his huge cock, the one glistening at the tip with his pre-come, and take it. I spread the liquid down his head to get it slick and shiny. When I lean back, he knows exactly what I'm after.

The predator lurking inside returns to his face. He puts one knee between my legs and nudges them apart, taking in what he sees there before he brings the head of his huge cock close. He runs his fingers over my clit again, and again, until I'm so ready for him that I'm whimpering.

The sharpness isn't immediate. At first, there's simply a pressure there between my legs where Raz'jin is entering me—and then it hits. I can't help the little cry of pain that comes out of me as his head pushes through. It's so huge that I'm not sure I can take him.

But he stops, just right there, and takes a few calming breaths. Then his hand travels down to my face.

"It's all right," he says.

And then he pushes in again, and somehow, he fits. I cry out with a mixture of pleasure and pain, and he smashes his mouth against mine. His tusks each tear a hole in the bed to either side of my face. Raz'jin continues on slowly, withdrawing just a little and then burying himself even deeper with the next thrust, over and over. I feel like he might tear me apart at the seams.

RAZ'JIN

I can tell by her voice that it hurts. There's no getting around that. But there's gratification there, too, as I sink all the way inside her—as far as I can get, anyway. Her body simply can't swallow all of me, but it doesn't matter. She's so perfectly tight, so hot and wet and squeezing all around me that I have to try hard not to come immediately.

I wait for her to adjust to me again before I pull out, and then shove myself inside her again. This is what I've always dreamed about, and it's everything I could have imagined and so much more. After a few more strokes, I notice the tears. They've started to stream down her face along the crease of her round cheeks, and I stop moving immediately.

Tel-eesa shakes her head. "Keep going," she whimpers out. She wants it as much as it hurts, too.

But I shouldn't drag this out. I pull her up as close to me as I can, so our bodies are flush, and thrust once, twice, three more times. It feels like the most perfect bliss I could have imagined. She's moaning while tears stream down her face, gripping me around the neck with all of the force in her entire body.

And then it hits me. I feel myself swell up fat, and she lets out a cry of surprise. Then I eject everything I have. She's so tight that it's like she's wringing me out, squeezing every last droplet out of me, and a low growl escapes me. I fill her up and more, until my seed is gushing out of her onto the bed.

We stay like that for some time, her body clenched around my cock like a vice. Slowly I withdraw it, and I know it must hurt like a bitch, but she doesn't make a sound.

I fall down to the bed next to her, and it creaks under my weight. I don't know what I expected the human to do after I just fucked her for the first time in her life, but rolling over and curling up close to my chest wasn't it. Her arms wind around my back, one of them down to my butt, which she has the gall to squeeze.

I chuckle into her hair. What a brave, foolish little human I've found. Who found me.

As she falls asleep between my arms, I have this feeling that I won't want to let her go again.

CHAPTER 8

TELISE

It was like the most exquisite torture possible.

I swallowed him up, as much as I could, and he filled me to a place I'd never imagined.

Now, my legs soaked in him, Raz'jin is gently running a hand down through my hair. His fingers stick in the occasional knot, but he combs it out without causing me any pain. It's such a soft gesture that I sink into his chest, where I can hear the slow, steady beating of his huge heart. Here, I can almost ignore the throbbing between my legs. Here, absolutely nothing can hurt me.

I fall asleep like that, just balled up in Raz'jin's huge arms. When I wake up to light coming in the one small window, a bit of drool has slid out of my lip onto one of those arms. But I'm not alone. My troll is dead asleep, like he's been knocked unconscious. It's amazing to see him so vulnerable. I could have cut his throat at any time in the night and stolen his beautiful emerald.

Eventually I have to move, and his eyes slowly open. They're soft, softer than I ever expected from a creature like him.

"Mmm," he mumbles out, yawning. "Good morning."

I repeat it back to him in Trollkin. "Good morning."

The sound of my voice seems to tickle him, because the side of his mouth goes up.

Eventually I do have to work, so I pry myself away and put my clothes back on. I wince a few times as I wriggle on the pants.

"Sorry," he says. I raise both eyebrows. What is he apologizing for? He makes an "O" shape with one hand, then pokes his finger through it, like a dick in a hole.

I have to laugh, and soon I'm buckled over and gasping at the renewed bolt of pain between my legs. Not sure how to say what I want to say in Trollkin, I just shrug my shoulders. Shit happens. That's life.

I'm not sure if he'll still be here later, but I certainly hope so. I want another round at least before he leaves Eyra Cove.

Raz'jin

Of course I don't leave.

You don't get your hands on the little nymph who ruled your fantasies for that long and let her go so quickly. Especially not one who has gifted you her first time in the blankets.

Soon I'll have to go—the weather is changing quickly—but not just yet. I plan to make myself at home for now.

"You having a go at that human?" It's the bartender around dinnertime. Why is he even talking to me?

"What business of yours?" I ask with a snarl.

He waves his hands. "No judgment here. This is Eyra Cove. People do what they want, if you know what I'm saying. But not that many human ladies who walk in here will hook up with a troll. That's a new one for me."

I stare him down, and the huge axe over my back seems to say what needs to be said, because the bartender backs away. "Meant nothing by it," he says, and goes back to washing mugs.

That's where she finds me when she returns that evening. Tel-eesa doesn't even approach me—simply beckons me from across the room, and then starts up the stairs.

Cheeky critter.

The first thing she does when we get behind closed doors is unbutton my pants, but I stop her one button in. "No," I say firmly, and she gives me a look like a pouty child. She's so adorable and yet so filthy at the same time I could just fuck her right then, but after the present she gave me... No, I'm going to take it easy on her.

Instead, I set her on the bed, and then pull off her pants myself without ripping a thing. She's already pink and wet between the legs. I can see where I damaged her last night and remember what I set out to do.

I pull her folds apart, and then lick her and lick her until she's trembling everywhere, and then lick her some more. I slide one finger in, gently. Almost right away she's gasping, clenching around my hand and spilling out onto my face. I lap her up, just drinking her in and relishing every drop.

This time I'm the one who's going to wring her dry.

Tel-eesa tries once again to get to my pants, so I let her. Before long she has her mouth on me, and I'm too helpless with the sensation to stop her. She swallows as much of me as she can, and the rest spills out around her mouth. It feels like a waste, but I'll get more chances to fill her up with me soon, once she heals. And then I want to jam as much of it inside her as I can. I want to fill up her belly with my seed until she's got at least one of my whelps inside her, fattening her up. Even though I know it's simply not possible for a human and a troll, that doesn't stop the instinctual part of me that's risen out of some deep, dark place and said, *this one is mine.*

I knew it when I woke up this morning with this little human wrapped up in my arms. She is mine, and only mine. She belongs to me now.

And so I make her come over and over again that night, until she's a twitching ball in my arms. She groans my name as she squeezes my finger tight, and I can barely wait until that's my cock again.

I'll take her every moment I possibly can, and I won't waste it.

TELISE

If I thought I was obsessed with the troll named Raz'jin before fucking him, that's nothing compared to this.

Whenever I'm at work, I'm thinking about him. As soon as I get back to my room he's there, slamming the door closed behind me. Advancing on me like an animal. Pushing me down against the bed and sliding down my pants so he can get his hands between my legs.

He's been waiting, I can tell, for me to heal. As much as he wants to sink his huge cock in me, he doesn't, patiently plea-suring me until I can't take any more. Who would have guessed a troll would be such an attentive and considerate lover? I always return the favor.

I'm surprised he's stayed around this long already. I

thought that certainly he would be on the next boat out, but it's already come and gone, and Raz'jin is still here.

In the evenings, after we've had a few beers—and more than a few stares—we retire to my room. Communication is still difficult, but I've decided to work on that. I found a few reams of paper and a quill, and I ask him to teach me. He's reluctant at first, but soon starts making rudimentary drawings to explain Trollkin words to me. There's no point in him learning Freysian; his mouth just isn't made for the more delicate, soft words. Not that it doesn't know how to be soft and delicate in other ways. He kisses me like I never imagined someone could kiss me—exploring my lips, nibbling on them, gently opening them to slip into my mouth. Sometimes when we're practicing Trollkin and he's trying to explain a more abstract concept to me, he stops to stare at my mouth. Without warning, he pushes the sheafs of paper and ink aside, spilling it across the table, then grabs me and crushes my lips against his.

As we're able to communicate better and better, I start to learn interesting things about Raz'jin. He's obsessed with my breasts. He thought about them constantly after he freed me that night. "I was drunk," he says. I'm glad he was because he might not have let me go otherwise. He makes the dick-in-the-hole gesture again. "Then that was all I wanted."

So it wasn't just me. I'm relieved to hear that he felt the same conflicting but overwhelming obsession that I did. Whatever had happened between us that day wasn't just a passing fancy. Some spark had been set upon the kindle, and now it was swelling into a raging fire.

When he can finally wedge two fingers inside me without inflicting any pain, my troll decides that I'm ready again. He's so eager that he's panting, but he takes his time to get me worked up. Now he knows exactly which motions of his tongue drive me wild, which way of touching me with his huge fingers gets me soaking wet and dripping onto his hand. This time, when he brings his enormous cock to my entrance, the head fits in a little easier. It still pulls me wide, and I have to grab onto his shoulders and bury my fingers in his flesh as he starts to push in deeper. It seems like there's no way it will fit, but then, somehow, it does. Not only does it slide into me, but once he's gotten the head inside, I feel a burst of pleasure I couldn't have fathomed.

"Do you like that, little one?" Raz'jin says, pausing his invasion to let me adjust. I can only nod my head and let out a whimper. He starts over, pulling the head back out and then slipping it in past that first wall, and I moan. It sends sparks flying up into my chest, my neck, even my face. He looks like he's just unlocked a secret door, and a wicked smile spreads across his face. He repeats the same motion, over and over, until I'm wriggling underneath him, begging for him to slide in deeper. I need him in a place I've never needed anyone before. I want to feel the real size of him; I want him to fill me all the way up until he hits that final wall, and then fuck me until I'm blue between the legs.

Raz'jin seems to sense what I want, because he takes a deep breath and drops to the bed on one elbow, carefully positioning himself for whatever is about to come next.

RAZ'JIN

I didn't think she could feel better wrapped around my cock than she did the first time, but somehow, she manages it. Teleesa is so soft, so wet, so gloriously hot around me that I have to work up every ounce of self-control not to sink myself as deep into her as I possibly can. No, I need to save that because once I do it, I don't think I could stop myself from coming immediately.

All of my careful attentions the last few days have paid off. She wants me so badly, and it's the greatest aphrodisiac possible. I want to give her everything she's asking for and more. I want to be her slave. I've never felt this way about a trolless or orcess before—like their pleasure is the greatest gift. But nothing sounds better than the human's cute little mewls, or her sweet, high-pitched moans as I start to sink deeper into her. How my cock can fit inside such a tiny thing is beyond my comprehension, but fit it does, and how perfectly.

Her legs wrap tight around my waist, pulling me in. Her eyes fall closed and her head tilts back, and I know she's enjoying herself as much as I am. Good. Very good. This is much better than watching the tears slip down the sides of her face. I want her to feel what I'm feeling, this same blissful, wire-tight tension. I want to make her gush around me like she does when I'm licking her tiny little pussy. So I continue my slow progress, finding each place that makes her clench up with pleasure and keeping myself there until she's a shivering, moaning mess underneath me, riding so close to her edge that a gentle push would tip her over.

That's when I finally go for the finish line and sink deep inside, as far as I'll fit. Maybe she can only take two-thirds of me, but it's enough to make my cock swell up even more, and it feels like every spare ounce of my blood is being siphoned there. She cries out, loudly, and I wonder how tired our neighbors are getting of her little screams.

"Good," she manages out. "Very good. Please." Her hands rise up to my tusks and there, she holds on for dear life.

I know what she wants. I pull back a few inches and then slide back in, trying to control the tension that's rising from my hips upward. I take her as deep as I can, pushing the limit more with every stroke. She cries out with each one, and when she pulls my face close to hers, I kiss her. It's the kind of long, deep kiss that I've only ever imagined sharing with a lifelong lover, holding her down to the earth while I'm buried deep inside her.

"It's here," she says in busted Trollkin, but I understand what she's saying. Her eyes roll back in her head, and her mouth goes utterly slack.

"Good. Give it to me." And she does. She screams out, and her incredible little cunt squeezes around my dick so hard I think it might choke me. I bury myself as deep as I can and then I'm there, too, everything inside me gushing out into her. She bites down on my lip, and I can't blame her because every one of her muscles is tight under my hands. I pump again, relishing the sensation of filling her up, of getting my seed deep inside her.

"Mine," I say to her as she trembles underneath me. I plan to fuck her many, many more times. Hundreds of times. Wherever I go next, she's coming with me. I can't possibly let her out of my sight again.

My mate. *Mine.*

CHAPTER 9

TELISE

"Mine," Raz'jin says, in the deepest, throatiest voice I've ever heard him use, right as he unleashes a massive stream of come inside me. It's like he's trying to get it as deep as he possibly can, and I eat it up, while the overflow spills out around us.

Mine. What does that mean? Is there some Trollkin implication that I don't grasp?

Because I'm no one's. I belong to myself—I always have, and I always will.

After Raz'jin cleans me up, he hefts me into his arms and carries me into the bath. There he scrubs me clean, from my neck down to the red spot between my legs. He washes it carefully, as if knowing how raw I am, and then moves on to my calves. It's such an intimate experience, to be washed by someone from head to toe.

When he's done, I repay the favor. I clean every inch of him, and his cock rises again in the water as I reach the sac between his legs. So this is where he stores it all up for me, I think, gently cupping them in my palms. Then I move up, cleaning the rest of his groin and his chest, and I have to admire the way he's built: He's thick and dense with muscle, and crisscrossed with scars. Some of them are significant, like the one that spans from his shoulder to his opposite ribcage, and I wonder what kind of injuries he's managed to survive. He's hardy and sturdy, I know that much.

Then I work my way to his hair and ask him with a combination of words and gestures to dunk his head under the water. I comb some soap through it, and then start to work out the tangles with my hands. He lies back between my legs and sighs deeply, his eyes closing. It's remarkable how relaxed he is with me, like some great weight has been lifted off of him. There's a part of me that feels like I'm supposed to be here, doing this with him, and it makes me itch.

That doesn't make any sense. He's a troll—just a weird, passing fancy of mine.

I push the feeling aside and keep working my way through his hair. But the unkept pieces around his forehead simply can't be tamed, and as soon as we're out of the bath, they dry and start shooting out again all over. It's really quite adorable.

A troll. Adorable. I'm really a freak.

More and more people are leaving every day as we start to get wind of cold weather. Though he doesn't say anything about it, I can tell Raz'jin is starting to grow restless. I have the sense that soon he's going to decide it's time to leave. And if that happens, I don't think I'll ever see him again.

That thought gives me pause. I don't know if I want to be separated from him, but I also can't leave Eyra Cove. Not now, while my apprenticeship is still in progress and I'm only two years away from my own master craftsman license. I would be sitting pretty for the rest of my life if I could get it. I'd buy all my materials wholesale, and occasionally do a hunt of my own, then hawk my wares in the city for a sizable profit.

Nothing in that plan accounts for Raz'jin. Nowhere in that life does he fit, and that feels deeply sad.

But I prepare myself anyway for the moment he decides to leave, knowing that it's coming like one of the waves that crashes against the rocky cliffs beyond the pier. I don't know what it will feel like to have to say goodbye to him, probably forever. Maybe he can return next spring when the seas are passable again, but I have my doubts that he will.

RAZ'JIN

The inn is slowly emptying out as the temperature drops. Soon the freezes will come, and then I won't be able to leave Eyra Cove for many more months. My dwindling reserve of coin wouldn't survive that. I have to return to Kalishagg and sell my emerald so I can buy food, and maybe a chunk of land somewhere to start building a home.

My time here is coming to an end, but I'm suddenly excited for what comes next. I'll throw my little Telise over my shoulder—I've finally got my mouth wrapped around her name the way she wraps hers around my cock—and then we'll climb aboard the last ship out. I don't know where I'll take her, maybe another contested territory. Anywhere I can keep her in bed and filled up with my seed.

Mine. I said it to her face. She must know my intentions by now. I've claimed her over and over, and everything in my body is telling me what my mind is just starting to grasp: This little human woman is my mate, the one I've spent my life craving without realizing I was craving it, and that means spending my remaining time on this forsaken land with her. Maybe I can't fill her up with little troll whelps the way all my instincts want, but I'll certainly try my hardest.

Telise's grasp of Trollkin improves every day, and it makes it much easier to live side-by-side when I can communicate with her. She's just as fiery when she can talk, making little demands and bossing me around—she loves when I jam one of my fingers into her ass and fuck her until she's sweating from every pore on her body. She's funny, too, and likes to make tasteless jokes in Trollkin when she learns new words. Her progress gives me even more hope for the future. Perhaps if I wrap her up in a hood and cloak, I could take her to Kalishagg with me, and pretend she's just a very unfortunate and secretive goblin. She's just learned the word "fuck" (I can't believe I didn't teach it to her sooner) when the first storm starts to blow in.

Shit. I've delayed too long and wasted too much time in this inn throwing back beer. Now it's really time to go.

That night, Telise sits astride me, riding my cock like it's an eager young horse. She likes it this way, where she can decide how much to take inside her and how fast. She uses her power for good and for evil, lifting herself up and down until I'm ready to explode, and then she stops, forcing me back into my own body.

I sit up, my hands finding their way to her breasts, then up to her face. I bring my mouth to hers and squeeze her body tight against mine, halting her movement. She gives me a look of confusion now that I've interrupted our flow.

"It's time," I say, pushing some of her long, red hair away from her face. It's disheveled and wild, just how I like it.

"Time for what?" she asks.

"To leave."

Her shoulders drop, and a look crosses her face that I don't like. She doesn't want to see me go, that much is obvious. I rub her back.

"You're coming, too," I say. I lift her up with my hands and start to move inside her again. "I'm keeping you. Forever."

Her expression changes again, and I'm surprised when I find it's not a happy one. She stops me with a hand on my arm, and slowly, disengages herself from me. But my cock is huge and swollen and covered in her, and it's desperate for release. I try to pull her back, but she isn't having any of it.

"No," she says, getting off the bed.

"No?" I reach out and grab her more firmly. I'm not going to let her wander off now. But she lets out a little hiss and buries her nails in my hands. I recoil.

"What's wrong with you?" I ask, incensed. She's clawed me before, but only ever when I'm inside her and her arms are wrapped around my neck. I have a number of long scratches across my back.

"No touch," she says. She still hasn't gotten a handle on the grammar yet. But she sits back down on the edge of the bed, just far enough away from me that I can't sweep her back up again into my lap.

She's never told me not to touch her. In fact, whenever I've touched her before, she melts into my hands like butter on a warm day. My Telise is pliable, soft, and as eager to be wrapped around me as I am around her. What have I done to earn this kind of insult?

My cock is starting to quiet down now that the atmosphere has shifted to something darker. Rather than touching her, I run my hand through her long hair, stopping at the knots like I always do to wrangle them out.

"Mine," I say again. I want her to say it, too.

But she just shakes her head and repeats, "No."

My mouth feels dry. When she looks up at me, her

eyebrows are drawn together the way she does whenever she encounters a word or a drawing she doesn't understand. "Not yours."

The low growl leaves my mouth before I know what I'm doing. Telise's frown deepens.

"What do you mean?" I ask. "Of course you are." Doesn't she understand? The way our bodies work together, how our spirits have chosen to tangle up as they have, it's obvious. She is supposed to be with me, to go where I go. We are linked now, inextricably.

But Telise simply shakes her head again and rises off the bed. "No. I'm not." She turns away so I can't see her face any longer and starts to put her pants on.

This isn't right. This isn't right at all.

First, the panic sets in. Then comes the anger. I get up and seize her by the shoulders, and she gasps at the power behind my grip. "Mine," I reinforce the word again, and lean down toward her so she can see that I'm quite serious. This is no game. This is my life. "My mate. Forever."

"Mate?" She repeats the word. It's one I've never taught her. I pull her waist against me and lean down, pressing my face to her hair. The way my tusks frame her head, it's like we were made for this.

"Mate. You and me. Forever. Mine." I don't know how else to convey it.

She pushes on my abdomen, hard, and I take a surprised step back. Her face is red, and her eyes are as sharp as razor blades. I don't understand why she's reacting this way. Doesn't she know?

Something shifts inside me as she refuses me again. It's a bone-deep kind of fury, that rises to the top like a dragon about to unleash hell.

CHAPTER 10

TELISE

Raz'jin keeps repeating this one word, as if saying it different times with different intonations will change the fact that I don't know what it means. But I'm getting an idea. "Wife," maybe? Whatever it is, I'm not interested.

I don't belong to him, and certainly not forever. Where did this idea even come from?

Don't get me wrong—I want him. I loved having him, over and over again. I enjoyed getting to know him, and learning from him, and spending time with him even when he wasn't sucking between my legs or driving into me with his cock. I have a very deep affection for him, that much is true.

But beyond that? It's not possible. I always knew it wasn't, and I thought he did, too. Now I'm starting to wonder how he thought this would end, and I'm concerned that the truth of the matter was not shared between us.

"No," Raz'jin growls. "Mine." He repeats the word again,

gesturing at me and then himself. He wants me to go with him, to leave Eyra Cove at his side on the last ship out of here before we're all frozen in for the winter.

And the more I push him away, the more I refuse to abide by this decision he's made—all on his own, I might add—the angrier he gets. I've only seen him this angry the once before, when I dropped from a tree branch and kicked him square in the head. When I held that knife to his throat, he had glared down at me with a look very much like this one.

We were clearly on completely different pages about what this relationship looked like and how it would end. That was a grievous error.

"You can stay," I say, gesturing to the room around us. "Stay with me."

The dark look in his eyes turns even darker. "I'm not staying."

"And I'm not going."

For a second, I see hurt flash across his face. He really expected something else out of this, that's obvious to me now. But that was foolish of him, and it's not my fault.

His hand clenches into a fist, and I wonder if perhaps he's going to attack me and try to drag me along with him anyway. He takes a threatening step towards me, and my hand drops to where my dagger would usually be at my waist—but I'm buck-ass naked. I retreat to the table beside the bed where it sits in its sheathe and reach for it.

Raz'jin's eyes widen as I take the dagger in my hand. I make it clear that if he's going to get violent, I'm going to get violent right back. I've defended myself against this troll once before and I can do it again.

It's like the dagger in my hand is the last straw. His face twists into rage, showing me a fury beyond anything I've seen before. He lunges for the dagger in my hand and wraps his fist around it, so the blade bites into his palm. I yelp, trying to pull the dagger free of his grip, but all I do is dig it deeper into his flesh. Some blood dribbles out and down his wrist. But it's as if he doesn't even feel it, the way that he uses the dagger in my hand to draw me towards him.

Then Raz'jin says something that I think means, "You're making a mistake." I yank the dagger free of his grip and he yowls, sending more blood splattering. As I back away, holding the dagger out with the point facing his chest, the yowl morphs into a roar. It's a sound I've only heard when ending a trollkin's life. He walks towards me until the point of my dagger is pressing into his chest.

"I'll do it," I say.

"I know." His gaze is conflicted for a moment, and for that moment, I can see that he's deeply wounded. But then the anger rushes back, and Raz'jin turns his head to one side to spit on the floor. He starts speaking words I don't know, so fast I can't even try to understand them. I catch *bitch*, and *fuck*. He turns away from me and storms over to the door, knocking over every single thing in his path. A table falls down, the one where we sat working on my Trollkin while he drew pictures for me, and he snaps it in half just by stomping on it.

"Stop it!" I yell at him. I'm going to have to pay for all this. "What the fuck?"

He turns around and bares all of his teeth at me. I'm so surprised by it that I freeze. He smashes his hand through the window, then turns on his heel and walks from the room.

What did I do to deserve all of this? He could have stayed here with me. It's not so bad, really, with a warm fire always burning in the belly of the inn. We could have had many more cold nights together, bundled up under furs and blankets, finding all sorts of activities to keep our blood running hot.

I stomp after him. "Raz'jin!" He pauses on the top step but

doesn't look up at me. I approach him and lower the dagger to show I'm not going to stab him through the back. I just want to touch him, to try to make him understand. But the moment my hand brushes his skin, he jerks away like he's been burned. Trying to push me off, he sweeps one arm so wide and with so much force that it flings me backwards against the wall.

"Asshole!" I did learn that one. He takes off down the stairs, and when I'm recovered from my collision, I race after him down. "You piece of shit."

"Fuck you." He's using that other version of the word "fuck," not the sexy kind, but the one that means, "I hope you get bitten by a snake while you're sleeping and die alone screaming." He turns to face me and jabs a finger in my face. "Liar. Traitor."

What? What did I ever lie to him about? He's taking this way too hard. I never promised him anything, and I certainly never lied about what I wanted out of this.

Every single pair of eyes in the inn is watching us have an incredibly ugly breakup.

"Fine," I say. "Get out." I walk up to the door and point the way outside, then switch back to Freysian, because I don't know how to say what I want to say. "Get on that fucking ship of yours and never, ever come back."

Raz'jin doesn't have to speak the same language to understand what I'm saying. He stomps over to the door and flings it open. I brush his hip with my hand one more time, and he pauses on the threshold as if he's about to change his mind.

But then, he doesn't, and Raz'jin storms out of my life for good.

RAZ'JIN

How could she have done this to me?

Telise led me to believe it was real—that what I felt for her was reciprocated. Maybe we didn't say it in so many words, but it had seemed so obvious to me. The way we kissed, how our bodies melded together like honey and bread, the happiness we both felt over the last month or more... I thought we had an understanding about what this was. We were mates, bonded together forever. Wherever I went, she would go, too.

It was the fear in her eyes when she reached for her dagger that sent me over the edge and into the abyss of rage. Not only did she not feel the same way about me, but she truly believed I might hurt her.

And didn't I? Ugh, I just meant to push her away, but she's so small that I sent her into a wall. Humiliating, really, to not know your own strength. Now all of that fear she felt is justified. That, perhaps, enrages me more than anything else.

I didn't mean to do it.

When I reach the dock, I'm so angry that I'm gasping for air. I want to tear my hair out, throw my axe through the wooden pier, scream and yell until I'm hoarse and mute.

"Are you, um, wanting to board?" asks an orc standing at the top of the ramp. He looks concerned at the state of me.

I glare at him, but then nod my head. "Yes."

"Transport for one?"

It should have been two. I nod again and hold out my coin. We exchange, and then I'm on the ship, ready to return to Kalishagg where things make sense.

After I've claimed a room in the cabin of the boat, I sit down on the bed and stare down at my hands. One is still bleeding, the droplets falling to the wooden floor and staining it an even darker brown. There are two long gashes now, one through my palm and one across my fingers where I grabbed her dagger and held it, hoping she would understand how hard I was willing to work to keep her.

But it all fell on deaf ears.

Later that night, the ship pulls away from shore. A light-house up on a distant cliff illuminates the sea. I come up onto the deck to watch as the little port of Eyra Cove starts to shrink into the distance.

For a moment, I think I see someone with bright red hair standing on the pier. But surely, it's just my imagination.

I'm one of the very few on board, as almost everyone else was wise enough to get out before the wind turned frigid. Now we'll have to contend with floating ice, and hope that we don't run into any of it in the dark of the night.

How could this have all gone so wrong? It boggles my mind that Telise would throw away everything like this. My rage is melting off and giving way to something else, something I don't want to even entertain.

No. Shame, remorse, sadness—those are not familiar feelings for me. In fact, they are far beneath me. But I can't help the swell of it anyway, deep in my chest. I remember when she showed me her cloak that first night in the inn, and I marveled at her craftsmanship. When I took out my most precious belonging and let her hold it in her hand.

I reach into my pocket to pull the emerald out and remember that moment right before we took the leap. I probably should have known, even then, that this was fated to turn out badly.

But it's not there. My jewel... It's not where it belongs.

On my way out the door of the inn, her hand brushed against my waist.

A cold fire starts to burn in the depths of my chest. No. She couldn't have.

As I replay it again, I realize that in fact, she did. Her shifty, quick little hand slid into my pocket and pulled my emerald out.

The flame explodes, filling my entire body. I want to jump into the frigid water and swim back to shore. She took everything from me, and I'm going to take it back. But the pier of Eyra Cove is already out of sight, just a flashing lighthouse off in the distance.

I roar and tear off the chunk of railing I was gripping tight in my hands. I could kill her right now, just reach out and grip her throat and squeeze until she goes limp.

For breaking me. For stealing from me. For ruining everything.

If I see her again, I will most certainly kill her.

CHAPTER 11

TELISE

His emerald.

I couldn't say exactly why I did it, I just did. Maybe I hoped he'd notice before the ship departed and be forced to come back, and then get trapped here by the ice. Maybe I wanted a piece of him—something to remember him by.

Oh, but now, with the ship long gone in the distance, I realize that he's definitely going to kill me the next time we see each other.

"I'm not going to be able to stay," I tell Sden the next day. "If that troll comes back, I'm dead."

He does not look surprised. "Word's gotten around," is all he says in response. Right. Very public breakup.

"Sorry." I put down my stitching. "I really wanted this."

"Yeah. You had the talent for it, too." He sighs. "Sex only ever gets in the way."

It was a mistake, I know that, but it was one I would easily choose to make again. After everything, I am glad I got to have him for as long as I did. It was a beautiful blip in time. Except that in the end, we just weren't after the same thing. I couldn't stand the idea of someone telling me what to do, where to go, who I was. How I felt about him was secondary. No, I had to stake my claim on myself.

But I do miss him, no surprises there. I know that I miss him the very first night after he leaves. I'd shared a bed with him ever since he'd arrived in Eyra Cove, and I'd grown accustomed to sleeping with his huge arm under my head like a pillow, the other one wrapped tight around me. Sometimes Raz'jin got hot during the night when we left the fire going and then he would sprawl out, legs taking up most of the bed, his arm still curled around me. Knowing these things about him, like how one of his toenails grows funny, or how he loves to be scratched right at the base of his neck—that's what hurts the most.

I have to sit with this for a long time and think it over, because I don't have much else to do outside of work. What did he really mean to me, after all? Now that Raz'jin is gone, it feels like there's a hole in my chest. I'm cold every night. It's like a bright candle has been extinguished.

I work hard for the rest of the winter, trying every day to lose myself in my daily tasks. But eventually we run out of raw materials, and the first ships won't be arriving for a few weeks still. We tidy up the shop, try to keep ourselves busy, but every day feels like one more step in an endless slog forward. Why do I always insist on spending winter miserable and up to my ass in snow?

As the ice starts to break apart and thaw out, it's finally time to run. For all I know Raz'jin got on the first ship back from Kalishagg, and one day soon he's going to stumble down the pier to Sden's shop and bring his hand axe to my throat, asking, *Where is my emerald?*

I pack up all of my gear, and as soon as the first ship comes in from Culberra, I'm on it. I drag everything back to the human city with me, and I feel like a dog with its tail between its legs. I find a note waiting for me at the post office from Deleran.

"I went back home," he wrote. "Whenever, or if ever, you want to meet me there."

I have to admit that after everything that's happened, I miss my friend. So the first thing I do is find a storage locker for all of my gear, then head to the train that will take me far out west. Once I'm in the king's city, it's a matter of taking a carriage the fifty miles to Great Oak.

I'm not looking forward to seeing my parents, but what can you do? Sometimes you have to go back home.

The whole trip I keep the emerald in my pocket, reaching in to turn it over in my hand whenever my thoughts stray back to Raz'jin. Sometimes I wonder what I could have done differently, but it all feels unavoidable, as if the cultural clash was bound to happen at some time or another.

It wasn't meant to be, and I knew that. I wish he had known it, too. Maybe we could have kept doing what we were doing until we grew tired of it.

But I have a feeling that would never happen.

My parents are shocked to see me when the carriage dumps me on their front doorstep. I haven't been home in a decade, not since Deleran and I left together to explore the world and find our place in it. My father is the first one to hug me. He's always been a softie.

"What brings you home?" Mom says, arms crossed. "You haven't even written to us in years."

Oops. I've just been getting in tussles, fucking trollkin, and almost dying while I was hung from my hands in an orc village. Not to mention ruining my apprenticeship because I couldn't bear to let Raz'jin go without taking a little memento for myself.

"Sorry," I say. "I've been busy."

"That's to be expected when you leave home to make it on your own." Dad gives Mom a look that says, *Come now, welcome our daughter home.* I can still read them like books. "What have you been doing with yourself? You look quite well."

It's the nice clothes and all the fish I ate while holed up in Eyra Cove. After making up a story that explains why I've temporarily left my successful craftsman's life behind, I go to find Deleran. He's probably bunking with his parents, too.

I wonder what brought him here. What trouble of his own is he escaping?

RAZ'JIN

I'd thought that by the time two weeks had passed and I returned to Kalishagg, at least some of the sting would have faded. But I'm just as furious as when I left Eyra Cove. I don't acknowledge the other thing, the deeper thing: The blinding hurt that lies inside my ribs like a lump of iron.

It's easy to find Blizzek, because he's sitting on the same stool at the bar as when I left. When I drag myself in, his eyes go wide.

"You look like you've been through hell," he says.

"Thanks for the warm welcome." I sigh as I order a drink of my own.

"So, did you find any?" he asks. I know what he means—

the emeralds I went to the Frattern Islands to find in the first place.

I want to tell him everything, but I can also predict exactly what he'll say and do in response, and that doesn't bring me any comfort.

"No. You were right. Pointless."

Blizzek squints at me. He clearly doesn't believe a word I'm saying, but he's never been the type to pry. "Not my business," he always says.

Much to my surprise, he's been seeing an orcess regularly, and that's why he's still here. But his coin is running out just like mine, and we both know that means it's time to cut ties and go prospecting again.

"The Southlands," I say immediately. I want to get as far away from contested territory as possible. I can't risk any chance of seeing her again. She wouldn't be foolish enough to stick around Eyra Cove after robbing me blind—she's not that stupid—so there's no point going back after the ice thaws. Besides, the south is a great place to spend the winter, as warm and humid as it stays nearly year-round.

Blizzek frowns. "The pickings will be slim."

"Maybe we won't hit it big, but we'll stay warm. There's day laborer work there, too."

"Day labor?" He studies me, like there's a mystery on my face he just has to figure out. "What the fuck happened, Raz?"

I've shown my ass. I haven't done day labor since I was a youngster just getting out into the world on my own. It was always beneath me to spend my days swinging a pickaxe at someone else's quarry, pulling out iron and coal to feed some other rich guy's family, or clear-cutting a great, magnificent mountain. Blizzek knows that isn't me.

But right now, I feel like I want to destroy something beautiful.

"I'll go with you," he says, "but I'm not doing any of that day laborer shit. That's all you, bud."

"Fine." I throw back my beer. "How's your lady going to take your leaving her?"

He shrugs. "It was never for keeps. I just didn't feel that thing, you know."

I know exactly what he means.

"Mate material," I supply.

"Right. Nothing like that."

I'm almost envious of him, to never have to feel what I feel now—the misery of finding that one, and then having it ripped away from you.

It's like Blizzek can read the words right off my face. "It's not worth it, Raz," he says, pretending like he's talking about himself. "All that mating shit, that's the old way. The way our parents did things. Not the way we do."

He's wrong. He just hasn't found his own other half yet.

"Sure," I say. "Of course. Let's go buy some train tickets, then."

It's the longest train trip I've ever taken. We pass the days playing Rampage, and I lose most of the coin I have left making bad bets. This puzzles Blizzek, too. I'm not usually such a poor player, but I keep betting everything on weak hands.

It's like the winter doesn't even exist this far south. When we finally step off the train, a warm wind hits me square in the face. The grasses seem to go on forever, ending at a green-blue sea. Huts dot the landscape, each with its own pasture full of sheep or cows or horses. It feels like rewinding in time.

We try to prospect, but the Southlands are a popular destination for freelancers of all kinds, and there's not much left to find. We hike far from the sea into the hills, using Blizzek's detector to see if we can find anything. We stumble across one thin vein of copper and even though it's almost worthless, it's better than nothing.

"This was a stupid trip," Blizzek says one night, chewing on his mutton. "All because you got your heart broken, huh?"

I freeze with my food halfway to my mouth.

"Yeah," he growls. "I knew it. I could practically smell the stink on you." I open my mouth to explain, but he waves a hand irritably. "No, you don't need to tell me anymore. I get it." He wipes his hands on his pants, spreading the grease around. "You've basically given up."

I suppose he's right. Nothing seems to carry much weight now. I could wander off into the wilderness and walk until I couldn't walk anymore, and then let a lion devour me, and it wouldn't make a difference.

"What's the point?" I ask. Women and money—that's all a troll wants. Now I have neither.

"Being alive is the point." But Blizzek isn't going to waste his time trying to comfort me. "You could always join the war effort if you're in the mood to die."

This idea, more than any other, sticks to me like a burr. Even after I wave him off dismissively, saying, "I'm not going to throw my life away in somebody's stupid political game," I know that it's exactly what I'm going to do.

CHAPTER 12

TELISE

"Wait, wait. You're telling me that not only did you fuck a troll, but he imprinted on you?" Deleran rubs his head as if this whole conversation has given him a devastating headache. "And then after your fight, you stole that from him?" He gestures at the emerald lying on the table between us.

"Yeah. I don't really know what I was thinking. It was just there, and..." I shrug. "It's beautiful, isn't it?" That's the only way I can explain the phantom that took over me when I stole it from Raz'jin. It's beautiful, just like he was.

"I'm surprised you haven't sold it yet. You could get by for a few years on the money that would bring in."

Defensively I pick up the emerald and slide it back into my pocket. "I'm not going to sell it."

He doesn't seem the least bit surprised by this. "Because it reminds you of him, doesn't it?"

I don't answer. It would just be opening myself up to ridicule.

Deleran sighs. "Why?" he asks. "Why didn't you just go with him?"

The question itself is insulting. "What do you mean? I don't belong to him. He doesn't own me. He could have stayed if he wanted me that bad."

"And you could have gone," Deleran says, "if you wanted him that bad."

"Well, I guess I didn't then, huh?"

But Deleran just looks at me with the most obnoxiously condescending, all-knowing expression possible. I want to beat it right off his face.

"Whatever," he says finally. "You came home. Why?"

It's a good question. I just feel like I needed a break after everything. I wanted to be somewhere familiar, somewhere that grounded me, so I would stop floating off into the sky.

"I missed you, I guess," I lie. But Deleran seems so pleased to hear this that he doesn't detect it.

"I think that's the first time you've ever said something sweet," he says. "Guess that troll really turned you inside-out."

"Can we not talk about that anymore?" I take a hefty drink of my wine.

Deleran's eyes are twinkling with mischief. "Of course. Whatever you want." He eyes my clothes. "You could make a fine living now. You really leveled up while you were gone."

That's true. Maybe I didn't get my master craftsman license, but the work I can produce is still valuable. The idea of it doesn't appeal to me at all.

No, I need to make a change in my life. If I keep walking the same path I was walking before Raz'jin, I worry I'll just meet him there again, walking the other direction. And that's the last thing I need.

We keep drinking long into the night, and Deleran edges closer and closer to me. I don't push him away. I'll take anything to get my mind off of the troll with blue skin and wild hair and gentle hands and a huge cock.

It's late and dark when we stumble into Deleran's house and make our way to his childhood room. I take off my own clothes, and he takes off his, and then we meet in the middle of the bed on our knees. Kissing him is sloppy and strange. I'm used to someone much taller.

Under his pants Deleran is generous, but nothing compared to my troll. He isn't gentle about sticking it inside me, and I only manage to orgasm by feverishly rubbing myself as he thrusts and moans and groans.

"Pull it out," I hiss at him as he reaches his climax. Hurriedly he obeys and dumps his load right on my belly. Once I've cleaned him off, I get up and start to put my clothes back on.

"You're leaving?" Deleran asks, and I detect a little bit of hurt in his voice.

"Shouldn't I?"

"My parents won't mind." A little smile tilts up his mouth. "They've been wanting me to settle down for years. I think you would be their first choice."

Who gives a fuck what his parents think? I try to smile back.

"It would just be too awkward," I say. "Maybe next time."

His face falls, but then he tries to mask it. "Right. Next time."

And there is a next time because I still desperately want to forget about Raz'jin. I carefully mix up some Purentea, made from the leaf of the Purennia plant, just in case Deleran forgets to pull out again.

We fuck all different kinds of ways, and his parents are certainly aware of it, but they have the tact not to say anything. Eventually I realize that I'm just using him, over and over, all while his feelings for me grow stronger.

Why can't I seem to stay out of this situation? I'm like a magnet for bad sexual partners.

"Could you imagine marrying me?" Deleran says one night after we've had a particularly long session. All I want is to feel that same fullness, that same rush of pleasure as when Raz'jin buried himself deep inside me, but it just won't come. Literally.

"Marry you?" I ask, too surprised to mask my disgust. "Um..."

Deleran sighs. "Yeah. Thought so." He sits up in bed. "You're still just trying to forget about him."

I drop my head. There's no reason to argue with his assumption because it's a correct one.

"I really didn't mind, not at first," he says. He approaches me and turns me by the shoulders to face him. "But now I'm starting to mind." Taking my chin in his hand, he tilts my face up to look at him, and I flash immediately to when Raz'jin held me this way, looked at me this way, and tears spring to my eyes.

It's the first time I've cried about him.

"Oh, Tea." He notes the water dribbling down my face. "I know you were hurt, but you did it to yourself, you know." I just nod. I know. "We have to stop doing this." I nod again. I know that, too. "All right," Deleran says, getting back into his bed. "Well, good night."

Like usual, I put on my clothes and head for the door. I feel like an era of my life is ending.

"I'm sorry," I manage to say.

"It's fine. I knew the whole time."

The next morning, I say goodbye to my parents. "You could stay for longer," Dad says. He doesn't want me to go. "I know you've been seeing Deleran. Maybe you should—"

"It's over," I say. "I don't love him like that."

Mom crosses her arms like she always does when she disapproves, which is often. "You don't have to love him to marry him."

Why is everyone so obsessed with settling me down? I want the opposite of that. I want to travel the entire world until I find the piece of me that's missing, wherever it might be, whatever it might be. I have to fill the hole that Raz'jin left behind or I might just die.

I say goodbye to my parents, but not to Deleran, then call a carriage. Soon I'm on the next train back to Culberra, poring over a map for where I'd like to go next. I could hunt spotted caribou up in the north, which have the most beautiful white pelts with brown dots, making them perfect for a rich woman's shawl. Or I could head south for the summer, to the Red Towers, where certainly no one else would be braving the weather during the hottest months of the year.

Yeah. Some suffering sounds right up my alley.

RAZ'JIN

I stand in line behind at least two hundred other trollkin, waiting for my chance at a bowl full of slop. Maybe it doesn't taste like much of anything, but it's nutrition, and nutrition is what I care about now.

We've been at this muddy camp for weeks, just waiting for the terrible rain to let up so we can advance on the human town forty miles from here. It's one of their last strongholds in this area, and they've been using it as a scout position. If we can wipe it out, they lose one of their sets of eyes. We could blind them.

I've killed not an insignificant number of humans since I joined up a few months ago. I keep hoping it will feel good, that it will fill up the gaping emptiness, but every time I cut off a head or bury my axe in one of their soft middles, I see Telise's face, instead. I kill her over and over, and every time it chips away another bit of my soul.

The war was supposed to help me forget her, not remind me of her constantly. But now I'm here and there's nothing I can do about it. If I leave, death would be my only reward for desertion.

So I slog onward, eating slop, freezing as I sleep under a hole-ridden tent, doing training exercises in the mud and rain. What kind of moronic decision was this?

And then, the rain finally stops. We pack up camp, sling our weapons across our backs, and trudge onward.

It's easy to take the town with the force we have, even though we're all tired and wet and some of us have trench foot. We lose more troops than we should have, given the circumstances, but our captain assures us this will be a turning point in the war. After this, we'll advance on the next town, slowly working our way towards the capital, where we'll meet the rest of the trollkin force. That's the plan, anyway.

If I'd stayed with Blizzek, at least I could still drown myself in drink and trolless pussy. But as it is I'm stuck here, trying to keep my boots dry and my axe sharp.

I dream about her frequently. Her little cries as she shivers underneath me; her big, toothy smile when she makes a filthy joke; the frightened look on her face when I told her, *Mine*, and grabbed the dagger with my bare hand.

As we advance onward, meeting greater resistance as we

go, I start to hope that some enterprising little human will make it through the front lines and stab me through the chest. Maybe then I could finally get some rest. Maybe then I could find some peace.

But there's a tiny part of me, the size of a pebble, that wants to keep going. That little nugget insists that I dig deeper and deeper into human land until I find her there. I don't know whether I'd kill her or spirit her away if I did, I just know that I want to see her face again before I finally die.

And yet, as we club our way through the human defenses, and more of my fellow soldiers fall at my side, there's no sign of her. I don't know what I expected, but of course she wouldn't be here. My Telise is a rogue, a hunter, and deeply independent to boot. She would never put her life on the line for someone else's cause.

I'm surprised at how much progress we've made when I finally come up for air again. We can almost see the capital on the horizon. Seizing the city would be like taking the queen in a chess match—all that would be left is the king, powerful but helpless. After that, little mongrels like Telise would become nothing but homeless prey, ripe to be picked off one by one until every sentient creature but trollkin are extinct.

And I have no choice in the matter but to keep walking, keep fighting, keep killing.

Soon I'm one of the few soldiers left in my unit, so I join another one. But then their numbers dwindle, too, until the ranks are suddenly refilled by a surprising abundance of new recruits.

They're young and agile, but also afraid. They are not soldiers like the rest of us.

"The Grand Chieftain has begun conscripting," one of them tells me, an orc that reminds me of a young Blizzek. "I was pulled off the street. Couldn't even tell my mother where I was going."

No wonder we're taking so much human territory now. It's no longer a choice about whether or not to join the war effort —it's an obligation under penalty of death.

CHAPTER 13

TELISE

The Red Towers are quiet, like I expected. I'm the only one walking among the great pillars of deep orange rock that spiral up into the sky. There are all sorts of creatures worth hunting here: Massive hyenas with gorgeous striped coats, elephants with huge tusks and thick leather hides, even birds of prey with supple feathers that make a pretty accent on any piece of clothing you could imagine.

For a while I can lose myself in tracking. I manage to take down a hyena with an arrow through the head—a perfect shot that doesn't damage any of the hide or fur. Once I have it skinned, I toss the corpse to some vultures sitting around stale water, and they scream and caw with glee.

After I've collected a hefty load of supplies in my pull cart, I venture back to the small outpost at the top of one of the many towers, which you can only reach by a big bucket attached to an impressive pulley system. I call up to request a ride, and it takes a good thirty minutes before anyone is near enough to hear me and pull me up.

The outpost itself is almost empty.

"What happened?" I ask the one guard posted at the guard tower. "Where is everyone?" Things have clearly changed in the weeks that I've been out hunting.

"War." His eyes look heavy. "Conscription."

"What?" I almost drop my bag.

"Every eligible man and woman not currently involved in a military operation," he gestures at his guard tower, "is required by law to return to the capital and join the war effort." Then he looks away from me. "Deserters punished by death."

My chest constricts. No. There's no way.

"Why?" I try to keep my voice steady as I think of Deleran, being dragged from his parents' home and stuffed into steel armor, a sword shoved into his hands.

"The trollkin are advancing quickly. It's not long before they reach the capital, so it's all hands on deck to keep them at bay."

Oh, fuck. A lot has changed just since I was home in Great Oak.

"I can pretend that I didn't see you," the guard says, surveying me. I just look like a pretty young thing with a cart full of supplies.

"Thank you." But if Deleran is going to be pulled into this, I have a responsibility to find him. To protect him, because he'll never be able to protect himself out there. "I'm going to enlist. Voluntarily."

The guard looks surprised, then a little sad. "You shouldn't," he says. "They're dying out there in numbers."

"I won't die." I'm too quick and too smart for that. "I'm just going to help a friend."

"Your friend is probably already dead."

I just have to hope he isn't right.

RAZ'JIN

We're only thirty miles from the capital when the tides change.

The humans must have begun conscripting, too, because their numbers suddenly surge. We meet a powerful resistance at the next town, and many of the new, young recruits fall at my side as we bludgeon our way through humans who look no older than children. Where I came to lose myself, instead I find a well of things to care about. I cleave another child through the head, watching his face fall in half in front of me. My axe is drenched in blood.

But we're still losing. There are more of them than there are of us. I'm one of the few left alive when our captain calls for a retreat. We fall back to our camp, where the human force wouldn't be so bold as to attack. We just have to sit and wait for the big guys to come up with a new plan.

That's when Blizzek arrives along with the next wave of conscripted recruits. I find him sitting around the fire one night, sipping up the same slop that I am. How he ended up here, when there are plenty of other fronts he could've been dragged to, is a mystery to me.

"Raz." He almost looks relieved to see me when I sit on the log beside him. "You're alive."

"Yup. Unfortunately. They got you, huh?"

"I came willingly. Didn't need to be told twice." He looks down into his bowl. "We're supposed to survive on this shit?"

"Welcome to war." At least I can trust Blizzek to keep himself alive, unlike these other whelps.

"Did you find her?" he asks. I furrow my brow. He still

remembers that? "You've said plenty without saying anything," he says at my expression. "There's only one little critter walking this land that could do all this to you."

I shrug my shoulders. "No sign."

"Maybe she's already dead."

This feels like a dagger to the heart. I imagine finding her somewhere face down in the mud, and that ball of iron in my ribcage starts to burn. I would find whoever did it and kill them, even if that ended in my death, too.

But at the same time, I can feel that he's wrong. No, she's still out there somewhere. If she were gone, I would know it, deep in my soul. There's still a chance to find her before we take the capital and the world falls at our feet.

"I'll keep an eye out," Blizzek says. He holds out his hand, and we shake. "It's an ugly thing, isn't it? All this." He gestures at the filthy camp, our dirty, blood-stained armor, and the bodies piled high in the woods nearby.

I don't have anything to say to that. It is ugly. It feels like if we win this, the world will come to an end.

My unit marches out the next day. The plan is to attack from both sides and burn their shoddy wooden defenses down with fire. I watch more and more of my fellow soldiers fall around me as a volley of arrows descend on us from the guard towers. I have a shield now, which I hold over my head as I slash again with my axe, bringing down another human whelp in thin leather armor.

Telise might be fast and clever, but eventually the war will find her, too. And when it does, she will fall just like the others.

TELISE

On the way back to Culberra, I'm surrounded by people carrying what weapons and armor they happened to have back home. There aren't enough supplies to arm all of us, so we're responsible for bringing what we need ourselves. Of all people, I run into Sden at the armory, where he's been conscripted into making what he can with the small supply of leather that remains.

"I could use an assistant," he says, offering me a very valuable non-combatant position in all of this. But I decline because I have to find Deleran. I can't let him face this alone. Sden just nods in understanding, like he expected this answer.

"You won't find him, by the way. The trollkin have conscripted, too. There are tens of thousands of them out there."

"Oh, I know." But there's a glimmer of hope in me, too. If Raz'jin were dead, I would feel it. That much is an absolute certainty to me.

I learned what that word means, from a book I read. "Mate." It wasn't just some fancy word for marriage—it meant a lot more than that. Like the book said, our souls were tied together on some other plane, and I can sense that his is still out there. Dirty and miserable and lonely, but out there, nonetheless.

But I don't get a chance to look for Deleran. I just have to go where I'm told, and I climb into a train car meant for hauling cargo along with a hundred other shivering humans. We're shipped like coal to one of the outposts around the capital city, where we'll act like fodder to keep the trollkin forces at bay. There doesn't seem to be any greater plan than playing defense. Our bodies will fall like so many dominoes, until our enemies finally storm the castle over a carpet made of our flesh.

When we finally reach our destination, we're split into squadrons. My first night in camp, I start to make my rounds looking for Deleran. I ask everyone I come across if they've seen the tall man with sharp blue eyes and a family crest shaped like a deer.

"Squad fourteen," a quiet woman says, and the life has clearly left her eyes. "I saw him. Kind of a hottie if you ask me. You his girlfriend?"

It's easier if I say "yes," so I do, and with her direction I find my way to where fourteen is holed up on the other side of town.

Sure enough, Deleran is there and still very much alive. When he sees me, he leaps to his feet and pulls me into his arms, and the familiar smell of him is surprisingly comforting.

"You're alive," he says, pushing my hair back from my face. He hugs me again, even tighter than the first time.

"For now. I haven't seen combat yet."

Deleran's face falls. "Oh. It's awful out there, Tea. You don't know just how bad until you see it with your own eyes." Then a little light reappears in him. "But it's not so hopeless as all that. There's a plan."

"A plan?" I'm glad to hear this. Maybe we could get out of this hellhole alive.

He gestures to something that just looked like a pile of wood to me. "Trebuchets. We've collected up all the steel left-over from battle—" he means armor and weapons scavenged off the dead, "—and it's been melted into shrapnel bombs. We drop a few of those on the trollkin and we can take out thirty, forty, fifty with a single shot."

Oh, no. What a terrible way to die. I imagine Raz'jin hit

with one of these, his body filling with shards of steel and falling to the ground in front of me.

Deleran reads my face. "Don't jump to conclusions yet. You don't know anything for sure. He could still be out there."

My troll is a clever bastard. He must have found a way to stay out of this.

"Find me on the battlefield," I tell Deleran. "I'm not letting you fight alone."

He smiles a little sadly. "That's the most romantic thing you've ever said to me."

Raz'jin

Despite our recent loss, our captains feel confident that our next assault will work. Maybe with enough bodies to throw at it, they'll be right, and we can finally take this forsaken place. And perhaps this time, I'll join the piles of the dead.

What we don't expect are the massive balls of steel the humans start to hurl into our ranks. I watch as they fall and explode, sending shrapnel flying in every possible direction. I'm only saved from it thanks to my shield being in the right place at the right time, but I can sense that elsewhere, Blizzek isn't so lucky.

Fifteen years I've traveled with him, all across the world, and now I don't know if I'll ever see him again.

The humans don't even bother to leave their fortress as they rain hell down on us. But I do my job and advance on the walls, bringing my fire to the kindle laid all along the base of it. The fire catches, swells, and quickly starts to spread. From up above I hear the sound of screaming. I listen closely to it, searching out anything familiar.

A spear falls from above, and I'm forced backwards. I rejoin the soldiers standing under the shelter of the trees, where we're partially protected from the shrapnel bombs falling on top of us, and watch as the fire spreads.

It's not long before the gates open and soldiers start streaming out. My eyes are riveted on them, searching their ranks for a familiar head of red hair, when another ball of steel is launched over the flaming wall. It lands right in front of us and blasts apart, showering us with bits and pieces of swords and spears and breastplates. One catches me in the leg, sending splitting pain across every possible intersection of my body.

These soldiers aren't here to fight us—they're here to collect and scavenge what remains of us.

I stumble backwards, blood streaming from my unprotected leg. Now I'll be here bleeding out until one of our enemies finally finds me and takes me prisoner or lets me die an excruciating death.

My leg can't hold me up any longer, and I fall back to the forest floor into a bundle of dense brush. The thorns tear at my face, but the branches soften the blow.

Already the blood loss is making my head swim. Humans shout as they fan out across the land, some of them trying to put out the fire, others searching for remaining combatants.

I've wanted to die so badly, and yet I've fought so hard to stay alive. Why? Once again, I drag myself into the brush so maybe they won't find me. Why am I clinging to life this way?

Because she's still out there, and, as long as I know that, I'm going to keep fighting.

The world starts to spin overhead, and then everything goes black.

CHAPTER 14

TELISE

I got lucky. My first day on the job and we score a big win. Well, *they* do, anyway—the people at the top who stand to benefit from this war. The more trollkin we kill, the more land we can snatch from them, and the big dogs can continue to expand their empires. Just how things have always been, and how they always will be.

The trollkin fell in great and terrible numbers, riddled with shrapnel. Most of them aren't dead, just bleeding out and dying slowly. It's now our job to find the dead and the living alike, scavenge what we can off of their bodies, then kill the dying and bring in the rest as prisoners.

Trollkin hate nothing more than being denied a valiant, honorable death.

As I step over bodies, each troll face I see looks like Raz'jin's. One of them grabs my ankle as I walk by.

"Death," she says. "Please."

I can understand her enough that I crouch down and say in

Trollkin, "I'm sorry." Then I bury my dagger in her chest. I wait until the life drains out of her eyes before I take what I can off her body and drag it to the pile of weapons and armor growing along the charred remains of the fortress wall.

Some of the trollkin retreated into the woods when the bomb fell, so I duck into the trees and start looking. There's blood everywhere, dribbling off of big leaves and pooling in crevices. The first two bodies I find are dead, with shrapnel to the head and throat. They had nothing to defend them—not a shard of metal on either of them. They weren't even properly armed.

That's when I spot a boot poking out from underneath some heavy brush. Something about that boot rings a distant bell. I crouch down and push the branches aside, hoping I'll find another dead body and not someone else I have to kill. Then I grab hold of the boot and pull.

First a leg emerges, and then another one. One leg is covered in blood, thanks to a huge chunk of sword buried in the flesh.

Blue flesh.

My hands start to tremble as I push away more brush.

No.

I grab him by the waist and pull as hard as I can, and soon, he's free. I take in his wild hair, his scratched-up tusks, and his familiar face. I know that face better than anyone's.

My Raz'jin.

He's unconscious, but alive—just barely. I have to hold back the tears that rush to my face as I search his body for any other wounds. Given the pool of blood around his leg, it's taking its toll on him. I look around to see if any other soldiers from my unit are nearby, but it's just me out here.

I don't want to hasten the blood loss, so I leave the sword where it is. I reach into my bag and pull out the first aid kit I was provided, and I almost drop all the pieces as I open it because my very arms are trembling.

He can't die out here. I won't let him.

I take out the cleaning solution and bandages. A woman on the train full of recruits taught us the basics: Remove the offending weapon, clean the wound, and bandage it up. That's really the best we can do out here on the field, but it should be enough to hold someone over until they can get proper medical attention.

But how can I possibly get him in front of anyone who could help? There's just no way.

I pull out the sword tip and quickly clean the wound. Luckily, Raz'jin is passed out, and I just hope it's not too late for him. If he died here...

I can't think about it. Focus, focus. Once I've cleaned the gaping hole in his calf, I grab a thick bandage and wind it around as many times and as tightly as I can. Blood starts to saturate it, but soon the flow slows down.

Finally the adrenaline catches up to me, and I fall to my knees next to Raz'jin's face. I push some of the wild hair away from his eyes.

"Please," I whisper to him in Trollkin. "Please, wake up." I reach into my pocket, where I still keep his emerald, then I grab his arm and press it into his hand. "See? I have it. I'm so sorry."

He's still breathing, but he doesn't move. I can't let one of the other members of my unit find him like this, so I kneel down and hook my hands under his armpits and start to pull. There has to be somewhere I can take him, somewhere we'll be safe until...

Until what? He's lost so much blood, there's a good chance he'll never wake up again. Maybe I'm wasting my time and my energy.

But I can't abandon him. Now that I've found him, there's no chance I'll leave his side again.

RAZ'JIN

I feel like I'm floating in a haze right above my body. The last of my life force is slowly draining out of me... Until suddenly it's not anymore.

Somebody is carrying me. No—dragging me. Who could that possibly be? Perhaps it's Blizzek, who somehow survived.

I can feel the rocks and branches tearing up my back as I'm moved, but the pain is dulled and far away. I'm drifting farther and farther from myself.

That's when I hear a voice: "Raz'jin?" I would know it anywhere. My body stops moving. "Please," my little human says. "Please, wake up."

If she wants me to do it, then I will.

Suddenly all the pain becomes exquisite and terrible. I can feel the gaping wound in my leg, the scratches and scrapes all along my back. I groan.

"Raz'jin!" Somebody takes my head in their soft, small hands. "You're all right."

Am I? But her broken Trollkin convinces me that it must be true. I open my eyes slowly, and when I do, I find familiar bright green eyes looking back at me. Relief washes across her face, and before I know what's happening, she's bent over and holding my head against her chest.

"What...?" I manage out the word, and my voice is hoarse. "Telise?"

I have to be dreaming. There's no way that she's real.

There's no way I'm lying on her lap, her breasts right in my face.

"It's me." She sits back up, and gently rests my head on her knees. She's smiling at me with the widest smile I've ever seen, huge tears dripping down her round cheeks. "It's me. I'm so sorry."

Sorry...? I blink a few more times, trying to get my bearings. Where are we? All I can make out is the dense cover of trees around us.

Wait. This woman...

This mongrel human threw me out. She stole from me. She's the reason I'm here at all. Isn't she?

I groan as I pull away from her, trying to support myself on my own.

"Raz'jin?" Her voice is less certain now. "Don't move."

I'm not going to let her tell me what to do, not after all this. "Ugh." I'm finally able to bring myself to a sitting position, and my leg screams in pain. "Where am I?"

"Your camp is that way. I hid you." She doesn't sound fluent, but she's able to get the message across. I taught her well. "Don't move your leg. It's hurt."

When I'm finally able to open my eyes again, I glance down at my calf, where there's a heap of bloody bandages wrapped around my wound. When I look up at her again, I know that Telise is the one who did this. She's the one who saved my life.

She should have just left me.

I glare at her. "Why are you here?"

Telise recoils a little, and her eyes are surprised. What did she expect? Some sort of happy reunion?

"War," is all she says. "Same as you."

Oh. So she got dragged into this mess, too. What's the chance that we would end up on the same front, fighting in the same battle?

I wish fate would stop fucking with me this way.

"Raz'jin?" She reaches up to touch the side of my face, but I grab her wrist in my hand and hold it at a distance. It seems to finally settle in her expression that this is not what she'd hoped it would be. But she doesn't know how long I've spent wading through the misery she caused me, the distances I've traveled trying to forget about her.

Her hand drops back to her side. Her tears haven't stopped, but they've gone from the happy kind to the sad. Telise wraps her arms around herself.

"I'm sorry," she says again, but no amount of apologies will make a difference to me. I've erected a tall, impenetrable wall around myself. Then she reaches into her pocket for something, and I wonder if she's going to whistle my position to her friends.

Instead, she pulls out a huge, green jewel. My emerald.

She holds it out to me, keeping her eyes on the forest floor. "Take it," she says. "It's yours." This time she doesn't try to apologize, as if she knows there's no apology in the world that can fix this. She just keeps her hand extended, the glimmering emerald sitting in the middle of her tiny palm. I reach out and take it, and the brief sensation of my fingers against her skin sends a spark up my arm. I know that skin so well, and what every last inch of it feels like. Now she's muddy and dirty and scratched up, but I can still make out the little freckles that cover her from head to toe.

I slide the emerald into my pocket and grunt as my leg moves. I'm not going to thank her for returning something she should never have taken in the first place.

But she didn't sell it. No, she held onto it for what, a year? More? It came into war with her, when she could have turned it into enough gold to sit pretty for some time. She could have bought her way out of conscription with this.

Telise kneels down in front of me, very near but not quite touching me. Seeing her up this close it's hard not to reach out and grab her, pull her in tight, and claim every part of her. *Mine.* That voice inside me won't stop repeating it.

"Raz'jin," she says, squeezing one hand tight inside the other, "I did not understand."

"Didn't understand what?" I ask, irritation in my voice. I can still remember the sharp ache in my chest when she insisted that there wasn't anything between us, the bite it took out of my soul when the ship pulled away from Eyra Cove that day and I discovered what she'd done.

"Mate," she says. "I didn't understand what you meant."

I thought I had made it pretty obvious.

"We don't have this," she says, gesturing to herself. "Humans. We don't mate. Not like you."

How barbaric. And yet they reproduce? And build cities?

"Foolish," I say. But maybe they aren't so foolish to not develop a bond like that, one that can't be broken. It could save so much pain.

"But you." She reaches out one hand so tentatively that I don't react. Her fingers land on my tusk, and I remember the way she thanked me the night that I freed her in the orc village. "You, Raz'jin... you are my mate."

Chapter 15

Telise

He's not happy to see me, I can tell that much. I might have saved his life, but to Raz'jin that's no exchange for what I did to him.

Of course, I didn't understand the link between us back then. He had known something truer and deeper existed there when I didn't. But even if I had fully grasped the implication of what he was saying, I wouldn't have been willing to admit the truth to myself anyway—that I couldn't live without him.

And, to be fair, he went about it all wrong.

But seeing him here and alive, no less, I finally get what that book about trollkin was trying to tell me.

"Some, but not all trollkin, mate for life," it had said. "The mating process is beyond simply electing to marry and unite households. It is a deep bonding between individuals—an imprinting of one mate on the other—that cannot be broken by time or space. It becomes a condition, and the well-being of one mate depends on the other."

I run my hand up and down Raz'jin's tusk, wishing more than anything that I could reach out and touch him. I swallow hard.

"But you..." I begin. "You are my mate." I say the word that I now understand means everything. All of this joy and bewilderment and heartache between us, because of this one word. "I'm sorry."

Now that I grasp the truth, the worst thing in the world would be if he turned me down. I've survived without him long enough to know that it's taken years off my life. Being near him now is the first time I've felt like myself since that night in Eyra Cove, and I don't want to keep doing this without him.

Raz'jin's eyes are unreadable and hard. I can see the same shadows of battle and death and fire reflected in them that I've seen. I realize now that he's only here because of me.

If he turns me away, I might as well walk into that trollkin camp with him and let the orcs finish the job they started. Now that I've found him and felt how it feels to be near him again, I have no reason to continue on alone.

"I'm sorry," I say, crumpling forward, the weight of everything finally pushing me to the ground. "But I know it now."

There's a full silence, and off in the distance, I can hear shouting, swords and shields clashing, people dying. It all feels so far away, like a whole different world from ours.

A heavy hand lands on my shoulder. Only Raz'jin runs that hot.

"Telise." His voice is thick and even more guttural than I'm used to. I raise my head and find him staring down at me with a sharpness, an intensity in his eyes I've never seen before. "You said, 'No.' Why?"

"I was scared."

He looks hurt by this. "Scared? Of me?"

"No. Of me." I didn't understand what was happening between us, what I was feeling or why. I press my hand to my chest. "It was new. Frightening. I wanted to be free and did not think you would let me."

Raz'jin's hard features, now decorated with even more scars than the last time I saw him, soften as he regards me. His hand travels up from my shoulder to my cheek, where he lets it rest. I lean against him, and relief washes over me just from feeling his skin against mine again.

"I understand now," he says, running his fingers up and into my hair, where he immediately starts to work out a tangle. "I'm sorry, too."

I take his other hand in both of mine and squeeze it as hard as I can. What I feel for this creature in front of me is so beyond love that it would feel idiotic to say it. I don't know how to in Trollkin—or if it's a word they even have. I wish I could say, "We both handled it badly," but that's beyond me. I turn his hand over to the twin scars now running down the inside and run my finger along them.

Raz'jin's other hand stops, then cups the back of my head and pulls me towards him. Soon we're chest to chest, our mouths less than an inch apart.

"You're mine," he says.

"You're mine, too," I answer. Then my lips meet his and everything feels like maybe it could be right again. Raz'jin grunts a little as his injured leg shifts under him, but then he kisses me even harder, his hands running down my neck, my arms, my hips, as if he might forget. They return to my chest, where he drags his fingers over my breasts through my armor. He stops at the side where my chest plate is strapped around me and unbuckles it without even looking.

He breaks away from the kiss and his eyes are ablaze, the

streak of red down the middle glowing like a flame. He pulls the chest plate up and over my head, and I know what he's going to do.

"But your leg," I say, and he silences me with another kiss, this one fiercer than the last one. He yanks my jerkin up and over my head, revealing my bare breasts to the entire forest. His lips find their way to one nipple, where he runs it between his teeth. It feels like diamonds having his mouth on me again. He sucks, hard, while his hands find their way to the buckles holding his pants up.

He can't be serious.

But Raz'jin is very serious. When he breaks away from me, he pulls his pants down, grunting with pain when they end up around his knees. Underneath, his cock is already big and ready for me, a trickle of liquid dribbling down the front.

I know what he wants, and I'm already wet for it.

I unbuckle my pants, and once they're off, I press my knees into the rocky forest floor to either side of him, getting pine needles and pebbles lodged in my skin. Raz'jin takes my jaw roughly in his hand and lifts my head, so I'm looking right into his eyes as he reaches beneath me and, with the utmost care, guides himself inside me.

Raz'jin

My Telise. My mate. I don't care how injured I am, she's mine and I'm going to claim her now.

But I'm hers, too. I understand now why she fought what I knew was true, and why it frightened her. She has a fire inside her and has won her own hard-fought battles. She belongs to me as much as I belong to her.

My human is staring at me with all of the ferocity in her small body as she lowers herself onto me. I watch in awe as her tiny, pink cunt swallows me up, one inch at a time. She's tight —so damn tight—and I grip her ass in my hands as she slowly rises back up again. My leg is burning, and the wound she fixed up has probably already opened, but I couldn't care any less. My cock has been aching for her for so long, and now that I have her, I'm going to do what I've been dying to do since the night I left Eyra Cove.

I reach down and rub her tiny clit, because I want to make sure she has the ride of her life even when I couldn't spend an hour preparing her for me. She cries out and then drops low onto me, letting me fill her up as full as her body will allow. I can already feel her growing tighter and tighter, sucking me inside and refusing to let me out.

"Yes," I whisper to her as she lifts herself up again, and again, and her little moans start to build. "I want all of it." She's moving faster, fucking me harder than she ever has before, hot breaths falling from her mouth with every lift of her hips.

And then she gives it to me. She sinks down as far as she can, and my cock vanishes inside her. She's moaning my name, tangling her hands in my hair, squeezing every last inch of me as she desperately keeps pumping. As she drips down me, I can't take anymore. I pull her down hard and drive myself into her as all the seed I've saved up for her comes rushing out. She moans and clenches and falls forward onto me, unable to hold herself up for even a moment longer. All I want is to pick her up and fuck her again, in every conceivable position, but this will have to do—for now.

I need to fix up this leg first.

When she's finally recovered enough to move properly, Telise climbs off of me and our shared come drips down her legs. I pull her down to the forest floor next to me, holding up her head with one arm. I know her skin is softer, more sensitive than mine—which wasn't particularly bothered by the pebbles and sticks burrowing into my back muscle—but I just need her close to me, if only for now.

After a while of stroking her soft red hair, I pause and say something I've been afraid to say.

"Neither of us can die," I say, taking her hand in mine.

She gives me a confused look. "It's war." She knows there's a very real chance that one or both of us may not escape this alive.

"If one of us dies, the other will go soon after." Her eyes fall to where our hands are clasped.

"Why?"

"Mates."

TELISE

Well, that's a downside I hadn't expected. But I should have.

After the pain I felt when we were apart, I can't imagine losing Raz'jin now. What would I do without the other half of my soul tethered to me?

"We should move," I say. "Away. Go away from here." It's the best I can manage in Trollkin.

"Where?"

I shake my head. I have no idea. But we can't stay here.

"I'll be killed," he says, along with a word I don't understand. But I know what he means: Desertion, if you get caught, is death.

It will be difficult with his one injured leg, but I believe we can do it.

I tug my clothes back on fast and help him get his own pants back up. The wound on his leg looks worse now, but the sounds of people are coming closer.

"Shit," I say in Freysian. I have to hide him. The human forces are still out here looking for survivors. "Behind tree," I say, pointing to it. It's bushy and close up against another tree. It should hide even him.

He crouches down and tucks inside the low tree, until he's invisible. "Shh," I say. "Quiet."

Just then, a few soldiers push through the nearby brush. It's three of Deleran's squadron, including him.

"You're alive, Tea!" He runs to me and pulls me into a hug. The other two soldiers with him raise their eyebrows. "What are you doing way out here?"

"One of them was injured. I chased him as far as I could, but he got away."

"Damn. An injured trollkin got one over on you? I'm surprised."

I shrug. "Lost my bow in the fray back there."

The other two roll their eyes and leave, looking for the next body to scavenge.

"C'mon," Deleran says, heading off after them. "Let's go."

"I'm not going."

He pauses at the tone of my voice and turns to me.

"What do you mean?" He lets out an uncomfortable little chuckle. "There's nothing out here, like you said."

"That's not, um, entirely true." I realize now that I can't get Raz'jin out of this alone. He's too big, and I'm not strong enough to help carry him out of the range of battle. "I found him. Out here."

"You found wh—" Before he can finish, I lean down near the tree.

"Raz'jin. Come out."

There's some muffled objection, but I gently tug on his arm. When he emerges from the tree, Deleran gasps.

"Human," says Raz'jin in Trollkin, leaning against the tree on one leg. He reaches for his hatchet.

"No, this one is okay," I assure him. "Good. He's good."

"I didn't know you spoke *their* language," Deleran says, eyes narrowed. "This is him, isn't it?"

I nod. "Yeah. This is him."

Raz'jin wraps his arm around me as Deleran takes in his injury.

"Ah, shit." My friend rubs the back of his head. "You want me to help, don't you?" I don't even have to speak for him to know. Deleran lets out a bone-deep sigh. "I could get killed for this."

"I know. I'm sorry." I'm putting my best friend in danger by asking him to risk his life for Raz'jin. But I don't have any other options. "Please."

Raz'jin growls as Deleran approaches, and he stops mid-step. "It's fine," I say to my troll. "He helps us."

"Help?" Raz'jin looks him over. "A human?"

"Good human." I nod again at Deleran, and in Freysian I say, "Can you hold up his other arm?"

"I can't believe I'm doing this," he mutters, but approaches Raz'jin anyway. Tentatively the troll lets him take his arm, and we start hobbling away into the trees.

Chapter 16

Raz'jin

I don't want to be helped by this "good" human just as much as he doesn't want to help me, but I can tell we're both doing it for her.

It's obvious from his posture, his scent, his voice, that he cares for my Telise, too. But she's mine, and he knows it.

They go back and forth in Freysian as we head away from the town and the camp. We're deep in the human lands, but the trollkin have taken almost all of the surrounding posts, leaving our own guards to keep watch. I have no idea whatsoever how we'll get out of this alive.

Telise suddenly stops us, and her keen senses are listening intently for something approaching. She points off in another direction, and we continue to move where her hand is guiding us. Finally she stops walking and holds up a finger.

"I will return," she says to me, and repeats the same thing to the human man. He looks even less pleased than I to be left alone together.

And then she's gone, silently moving through the trees. Clever thing.

We sit and wait for what feels like far too long. Has she been caught? And then, like a shadow from the mist, Telise reappears. She nods and points.

"This way," she says, then repeats the directions to the other human. The three of us start to move again and soon we come upon a small farm. The occupants have all fled, and it's not important enough of a landmark to have a guard. Inside a pen are two horses past their prime. But they have four legs, and they can carry us a good way.

We saddle them up, and when it's time, the man helps me up onto the larger horse. It's just as undignified for him as it is for me, and that brings me a modicum of pleasure.

Before Telise gets up on her own horse, the other human hugs her. I bristle, but I know he's not coming with us. Anyway, there's no reason to be jealous—at the end of the day, she'll always be mine.

And then we're off. The man waves a few times, then ducks back into the woods.

We stay off the main road, keeping to the tree line so we can't be easily seen from passers-by. We come to a stop and stay out of sight as a small patrol of trollkin march past, and then continue on our way.

Settlements thin out the farther we get from the capital, and the invasion has forced out any humans who might have remained. We stop in multiple abandoned homes to pick up supplies, and Telise cleans and re-dresses my wound. Then we continue on again.

We spend nights curled up in what furs we could find and carry with us, looking up at the stars. I can't get proper medical attention on my leg, so I can already tell it's healing wrong, but there's nothing we can do about it in the meantime. At least it's clean and not infected.

There's nowhere we can go, a troll and a human. Soon the human lands give way to the hilly, brush-covered plains. The horses are tired after days and days of walking, and so are we. Eventually we find a river flowing with clean, cool water, both sides rimmed by tall trees. I can almost put weight on my leg again, so we take off our clothes and bathe. Well, bathing is one of the things we do. The horses give us odd looks as I take Telise against one of the riverbanks, lapping her up with my mouth before I slide into her from behind. She bends over, moaning my name, and I wait until she's good and ready to burst before I empty myself inside her. I shove it as deep as I can, wondering if maybe this time, if I just try a little bit harder, I can fill her up with one of my whelps.

One afternoon, we're spotted by a group of three humans. They see Telise first and ride towards us, calling out pleasantries—until they see me riding beside her, and start to pull out their weapons. But Telise is moving already. She leaps off her horse, one arrow flying. It takes out the first human in the chest, and then she unleashes another. As both arrows land in their targets, she vaults off the ground and takes out the last human with a dagger to the throat.

I watch all of this happen, of course, from the safety of my horse. She's fast and deadly, and I'm just glad that she's on my side. If it hadn't been for Blizzek and his blunderbuss that day, I would be dead.

She also just murdered three of her kinsmen to make sure they wouldn't hurt me, and that touches me more deeply than anything.

I would kill anyone for my Telise, but I'm not sure if I'll ever have the chance again.

TELISE

Soon the plains give way to the hilly lands of the Sandteeth. How strange that everything comes full circle.

We're out of food now, so it's up to me to hunt when I can. But Raz'jin is no slouch at skinning and butchering, and we take a few days to give the horses a rest and dry out some extra meat. We've been walking for weeks now, avoiding travelers who might be on the main road.

But our luck can't hold out forever. We need a plan, somewhere to go, away from the war.

We still have the emerald with us, so when we reach the nearest trollkin-controlled port, Raz'jin goes looking for someone who would be willing to carry us safely—and privately—to the Frattern Islands.

It's the best place I can think of for a human woman and her injured troll lover to go, where there will be no human guards to call me deserter and try to chop off my head.

Raz'jin is able to secure passage with a fellow troll merchant. He must have warned his countryman about me, because once we're aboard the ship, Raz takes my hood off.

"Damn," the other troll says, shaking his head. "Never seen anything like this, I'll tell ya that."

But one whole emerald was enough to shut him up, for now and for good. He treats us like first class passengers the entire three-week passage, even when he has to listen to us fucking late into the night.

Raz'jin and I both know that his leg will never quite recover, but at least he can walk now on his own, albeit with a limp.

"Go on, you strange kids," the merchant says when we finally make land at Eyra Cove. "Go do whatever it is you do."

Without the emerald, neither of us has much in the way of coin, but Sden's old shop is empty and has a nice room up above it.

"Can you stay here alone?" I ask one night, as we eat some of the last food we can afford to buy.

"I'm not an invalid," Raz says, getting up to his feet as if to prove his point.

"Invalid?" I ask. He explains the word to me. "Ah. I didn't think you were. But I'm going to leave for a long time."

He frowns deeply. "Where? Why?"

"Hunting." I need some way to make a living, and I only know of one way to do it. I also have gear and supplies hidden away in Culberra. As soon as the war is over, I'm going to make my way back there and retrieve it.

Raz spits into the fire. "I should be going with you." I know it hurts his self-esteem to sit here and wait helplessly for me to come back, and there's nothing I can say that will help. Even if he didn't have a busted leg, he would be too loud for what I need to do.

"Wait for me," I say, kissing his head. He pulls me down into his lap and bundles me up in his arms, encircling me completely.

"Always."

RAZ'JIN

It's a terrible thing to be without your other half, especially when that other half is putting her life on the line so you might survive.

But I know my human will return safely, because if anyone can take care of herself, it's Telise.

The war goes on and on. I find myself at the inn frequently since I have little else to do. The same bartender is there, but with spending so much time alone, I don't mind his prying questions.

"So you made up," he says with a chuckle while serving my beer.

I shrug. "Mates, you know?"

His eyes widen. "With a human?"

"When it happens, it happens."

He doesn't look as disgusted as I expected, more perplexed.

"Huh," he says. "Never know what you're going to find in this place."

I spend a few days searching the coastline for emeralds, but I don't see another like the one Telise carried in her pocket all that time. When I get back to Eyra Cove and the little leather shop, it looks like a hurricane has blown through.

"Raz?!" When I walk in the door, I'm almost bowled over by a small creature with her arms thrown around my neck. My Telise.

"You're back," I say. "I didn't expect you yet."

She's angry, relieved, and enamored all at once. "I told you to wait!"

"I'm sorry." She kisses me hard, and I return it just as fiercely. Then I pull a little rock out of my pocket. "I found this, though."

I produce a tiny round object—a pearl. It's no emerald, but it's nothing to sneeze at, either. Telise takes it in her hand and holds it up to the light.

"Oh! It's perfect. I know exactly where it should go." She leads me to the back room, where she's spread out all of her findings. There are beautiful hides of all sorts. She was busy.

"Look at this." She pulls out a beautiful lion hide, the fur as smooth as silk and the mane bushy and full. She mimics tying it around her throat, holding the pearl up in the front. "What do you think?"

I wrap my arms around her, and she catches the pearl in her hand just in time.

"It's beautiful," I say, pulling her close. She gets that mischievous look in her eye that she only gets when she's about to tear off all my clothes. She's been gone for almost three months, and I'm more than ready to reclaim her. But I'm going to take my time about it and show her just how much I missed her.

I take off her clothes one item at a time, until she's standing naked in front of me. Something about her looks different, but I can't quite put my finger on it.

I push her against the bed, then fall to my knees in front of her. I'm going to remind her what it means to be home with me again.

At first, I tease just the outside of her with my fingers, and then bring my tongue to the tiny bundle of nerves right above her tight little slit. How she still looks so fragile and small after the way I've taken her... It mystifies me.

Soon she's moaning under my mouth, so I add one finger, and then two, until I'm licking her and pumping my fingers inside her, and she's crying for mercy. Just before she falls off the edge, I stop, and she gasps with indignation.

I waggle a finger at her. "Not yet." When I move up her body, though, I see something new. Her belly is less flat than I remember, and there are spiderwebs of pink lines sweeping up across it. "Hmm," I say, kissing her there. "What's this? Ate too many blueberries while you were out hunting lions?"

She doesn't laugh at my joke. Okay, sure, it wasn't a very good one, but—

"I think you can guess what it is," she says quietly. And when I look up at her serious face, it strikes me like a bolt of lightning.

"It can't be." I take a step back, soaking in the sight of her. Her belly is most definitely more swollen than it was when she left. Her breasts look a little bigger than I remember, and there's a new roundness to her cheeks, too. They're pink and shining.

At first, it feels like I've won some impossible prize. I've done it—we've done it. Now there's one, maybe even two of my whelps growing inside her. I want to bury my face in her tits, and then sink my cock deep into her and take her over and over again until she can't come around me even once more.

And then I take in the concern on her face, and I have to back up.

Wait. What does any of this mean?

"Is it mine?" I ask, suddenly feeling suspicious. She was gone for a long time. And that other human, whatever his name had been—I know how he felt about her.

Before I can finish the thought, Telise whacks me across the head. "Ow!" I clutch my ear. "That hurt."

"Of course it's yours, you moron." But she's cautiously smiling. "I just didn't think it was possible." There are so many unasked questions on her lips, ones that I have no idea how to answer. "How?"

I just shake my head. There's probably not a lot of scientific study in this particular area. But I did hear, once upon a time, that trollkin and humans descended from one shared ancestor.

"I don't know. But it's amazing." I feel across her belly and imagine the little creature growing inside there.

"Is it?" She doesn't look so convinced. "What will it be? Will I be able to..." She doesn't want to finish this sentence.

She's tiny—small enough to look like a large troll child. What would carrying my whelp do to her?

I'm starting to understand her worry, but I brush it off for now. "It'll be fine," I say, returning to my devotional. I'm going to make her feel so good that she'll never want to leave me again. "It wouldn't have worked if it wasn't going to be all right."

And for now, she believes me, because what other choice do we have?

CHAPTER 17

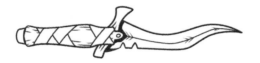

TELISE

Raz'jin is much more delicate with my breasts now that he knows. He covers my entire body with his lips, tasting every last inch of me. I try to bring his huge cock to my mouth and lick him up, but he shakes his head.

"I'm going to fuck you so many times that everyone in the city will hear you," he whispers in my ear as he presses me down on the bed. "I'm saving it all up for you."

He pulls me to my knees and, once my ass is up in the air, he fills me with his tongue. He's intent on his mission, and I won't stop him.

Now that I'm wet and dripping, he starts to rub the head of his cock against my clit, over and over, until I'm whimpering. "I want it, Raz. Please."

"What was that?" He stops to put a finger inside me, testing me out, exciting me. "Tell me again."

"I want you inside me."

He brings his cock back to my entrance and gently presses

his head inside. But then he retreats again, rubbing back and forth, over and over, until I'm begging for him.

"All right," he says, and starts to slide in from behind me. He's impossibly big, like always—and just like always, he manages to fit, spreading me as wide as I can go. Every small stroke is like a spark being tossed onto kindle. Just when it feels like I'm about to come around him, Raz slows down, and I'm left moaning.

Then he continues on again, assuring me that he'll let me have my release soon. He's coiling me tighter and tighter, until I'm so wound up that I feel like I'm going to explode.

"Yes," he whispers in my ear, and starts to move harder, faster. He lifts all of me up in his arms, and it's like I weigh nothing to him. He finds my magic spot, the place inside me that only he knows how to find, and it's the bolt of lightning from the sky I needed to light on fire.

When I finally reach the top, I burst around him. Raz moans and bites into my shoulder, his tusks cradling either side of my head. As my juices coat both of us, he starts moving again. Usually by now he can't hold it in anymore, but he must have practiced his stamina while I was away.

He continues to fuck me long into the night, until finally he gushes inside me, groaning out my name. He buries his cock as deep as it'll go, and I have to chuckle to myself.

"You already put one in there," I say as he pulls me into his arms, still inside of me. He grunts against the top of my head.

"Yeah, but what about after that? Then I'll have to fill you up with another one."

"Aren't you getting ahead of yourself?"

He shrugs. "Just making sure I'm doing my job properly."

But we can't pretend everything is dandelions forever. We get word that the war is finally over. The capital never fell, and eventually the trollkin had to withdraw. They were spread too thin and didn't have enough forces to keep a hold on their claims and continue their assault at the same time.

We're back to square one, with thousands—maybe tens of thousands—more dead bodies to show for it.

That means Sden will be returning soon, and I can get my missing supplies.

"I don't think you should go," Raz says. My belly is a lot rounder than it was when I first returned, but I'm almost out of leather to work into sellable pieces.

"I know. But I have to."

He makes that face he always does when I'm right and he doesn't like it. "I'll be back soon, and then you can fuss over me all you want."

I know exactly what kind of dad Raz'jin is going to be, that's for sure.

But I worry the whole journey back to Culberra about what this means for us, for me, and for this little creature growing inside me. I have nightmares that it comes out a monster, deformed and broken. But nature would never let that happen, right?

Once I'm in the city, I inquire around all of Deleran's favorite watering holes. Someone points me to his room at the inn. Just before I knock on the door, I pause my hand. What will he do, say, and think when he sees me?

I drop my hand to my side. He helped Raz and I before, but I don't know how far that grace extends.

"Tea?"

I turn around to find Deleran in the hallway, holding his key out. He's hugging me before he can even get a good look at me. "You're back!" he says buoyantly, sweeping me up into the air.

"Wait," I say. "Put me down." Everything is sloshing around inside me, and it makes me feel sick.

"Huh?" When he drops me to my feet, he takes in the state of me, and his eyes go wider than I've ever seen them. "This can't be real."

"It is."

He wipes his forehead. "You've always been a freak. Now you're a freak of nature, too." But I can hear the little sprinkle of affection in his voice as he says it. "Why don't I buy you something to eat, since you're eating for two now?"

I'm surprised by his offer, but pleasantly so. When we sit down together, Deleran wants to know what happened after the last time I saw him. But the longer I talk, the sadder his expression gets. I feel like all I'm doing is driving the needle in deeper and twisting it around.

"I'm happy for you," Deleran says, forcing out a big smile. "You found what you wanted after all."

"I hope you can find what you want, too," I say. He just watches me, head propped up on one elbow, the resignation clear on his face.

"Yeah," he says, but the word is empty. "Me, too." I feel ashamed for coming to visit him at all, knowing how he still holds a candle for me. But then Deleran says, "I'm glad I got to see you. I'm glad that you found him again."

"Thank you." When we get up after our meal, he studies me.

"Can I touch it?" I'm surprised that he's asking, but I nod, and he reaches out to run his hand over my swollen belly. "Wow. I didn't think it was possible. Are you going to be okay?"

"I hope so." That's all I can do, anyway, is hope.

"Take care of yourself, Tea." He smiles forlornly. "Maybe I should find some lady orc of my own, huh?"

"If you're into that kind of thing." The thought of a big orcess pushing him down and having her way with him does make me giggle a little. "You might like it."

"I'll think about it."

"Thanks for everything," I tell him. And I mean it. Without Deleran, we might never have made it. But when we hug good-bye, I think it's probably the last time I'll ever see him.

RAZ'JIN

It's a pretty awkward reunion when the shop owner returns and I'm, well, living in his shop. But after some hurried expla-nations and a look around at all of Telise's wares, old Sden seems to accept that I'm telling the truth.

"Weird shit," I hear him mumble. "Well, you all had better look for a new place to live."

He's doubly shocked when Telise returns home, full to bursting. I'm a little concerned at how big it's grown and how quickly.

"On second thought," Sden says, "maybe you should stay for a while."

He makes us comfortable in the back of the shop, and I help out as much as I can. Telise is able to earn our keep for the most part, until she starts to hurt. There's no position she can lie in that doesn't feel deeply uncomfortable, and I'm starting to get worried.

Scratch that—I'm terribly worried, and there's nothing I can do about it.

There are healers who pass through from time to time, and I wait every day on the pier for someone to arrive. When an old human woman gets off the boat in a healer's cloak, I jingle some coins, and bring her as fast as I can to Telise's side.

She looks between us with an expression I've gotten quite familiar with, landing somewhere between shock and horror.

She points at me, and rattles off some Freysian to Telise, who just nods in return.

I think the old healer is afraid for Telise, too, because she sticks around for more than just a few days. Sden grows annoyed with all the company and eventually moves out himself to live at the inn. I've really grown fond of that grumpy old man.

"She thinks it will be all right," Telise tells me, even though the healer's face does not scream *everything is golden*. "It's just going to come out a lot sooner than we expected."

Oh. Well, that would be a good thing, wouldn't it?

I'm headed back from the shop around the corner when I hear her screaming.

TELISE

It just starts to happen all at once.

The healer had told me I would feel a few initial shocks before my labor started in earnest, and then it would be a long, drawn-out process. Instead, it is like my body is suddenly saying, *It's done!*

Trying to squeeze out a huge, half-troll baby is most certainly the most excruciating thing I've ever experienced, but seeing Raz running in the door takes me out of it for the briefest moment. He crouches down by the bed, holding my five fingers in his four.

"Four or five, do you think?" he asks, pushing some sweaty hair away from my face.

It takes me a moment to realize what he's asking, and I manage to laugh between gasps. "Five."

"Bet."

The old healer goes into action. She coaches me as best she can through my screaming. When the pain becomes more than I can possibly bear, I grab Raz by the collar of his shirt and curse him and his huge, evil cock for putting this baby inside me, but he just smiles and runs a cold cloth over my face. I could kill him.

"She's starting to lose some blood," the healer says. But he can't understand her, and I can't translate through the fog of agony. I feel my body becoming weaker each time I try to push, and Raz's face is growing more concerned as the healer brings over more and more cloths, most of which come away red.

"Telise?" He squeezes my hand tighter. "Stay with me, please."

It's only thanks to that hand inside mine that I manage to push through a pain greater than anything I thought I could possibly bear. But it does end, eventually. The healer lets out a huge sigh of relief, and carries a small bundle wrapped in fur over to me.

He is much more familiar than I was expecting. His skin is light blue, like the sky, and he already has a smattering of messy red hair. He has four fingers.

"No tusks?" I ask. I'd been terrified of that part.

"Not until we grow up a little," Raz says, grinning like a fool.

Soon the infant is all dried off, and then we figure out the whole suckling business. Raz leans forward on the bed until he's sprawled across it, his head on my thigh, and strokes the little creature's back.

"Looks just like a troll whelp," he says with surprise.

The healer woman looks the most relieved she's ever been in her life. She packs up her things right away and leaves us to our devices.

That night, Raz kisses down the side of my face, his arms running along my hips while the baby sleeps against my chest.

"I wasn't joking when I said that about your dick," I say. "You get that thing near me again and you're dead."

He laughs and holds up his hands in surrender. "No promises."

RAZ'JIN

Izzek grows like you would expect any other little troll to grow. His tusks take time to emerge, but they'll be impressive someday. He cries and sucks his mother's breast like any baby would, even if he's a bit bigger.

I make myself useful building a new attachment onto the back of the leather shop while Telise works, carrying Izzek around in a holster on my back while I fit wood together and hammer in nails. Sometimes he needs his mom, and then he rolls around on the floor while she works on her leathers or tries to sell wares to a customer. The people of Eyra Cove have seen every odd thing on the block, so there's really no reason to hide our way of life here as long as we pay our taxes. Newcomers stare, but we get used to it.

Now I have everything I never even knew I wanted, bad leg and all.

Telise does forgive me and my cock both, of course. Though as hard as I work at it, I can't seem to put another whelp inside her. But I'll sure as hell die trying.

JOIN MY NEWSLETTER!

For all the latest regarding books, and to get access to a free extended epilogue that continues Telise and Raz'jin's story (and Izzek's!), sign up for my newsletter!

www.LyonneRiley.com

Also by Lyonne Riley

Trollkin Lovers

Healing the Orc's Heart

Tales of Monstrous Romance

Prince of Beasts

ABOUT THE AUTHOR

I come from a traditional publishing background, which is rewarding but often rigid. Most traditional publishers are not looking for books where pretty young virgins fall in love with monstrous trolls and have lots of sexy times, so I shifted to self-publishing to pursue my real passion in writing. I probably should have known I would end up here after spending most of my young adulthood writing erotic fan fiction about monsters, but it took me a while to find my way back to myself.

ACKNOWLEDGMENTS

I would like to thank everyone involved in helping me through the process of putting out my first self-published book. This was a rocky road, and I can't say enough how much I appreciate the help and encouragement of the people around me. Thank you to Amber, who suggested I try this out in the first place. Huge thanks to my cover artist, Rowan Woodcock, who brought Telise and Raz'jin to life. Thank you to my friend Keith for creating the spot illustrations that decorate this book. To my critique partners, especially Ruth, who give me phenomenal editorial feedback: You all make this possible. And of course, my amazing spouse, who has always supported my dreams—and given me lots of inspiration for my characters' sexy adventures.

I couldn't have done this without the expertise of my fellow self-published romance authors, Chace Verity and Pamela DuMond. Thank you for inviting me into your circles and helping me through this process.

And thank you to my readers, who gave this book a shot.

Made in the USA
Las Vegas, NV
21 January 2024

84720497R00079